"My hero."

She put her hands around his waist and hugged him tight, then reached up and kissed his cheek. She'd intended to keep things light, but when her lips touched his warm skin, electricity shot through her body, stunning her with its intensity. It was like grabbing a live wire. She sucked in a breath and got a whiff of his heady scent mingled with a hint of aftershave. He smelled so good. Their eyes met and held and sexual attraction arced between them.

He wrapped his arms around her waist and pulled her more closely to him. She leaned her head against his chest, feeling the steady beat of his heart beneath his cotton shirt. It felt so good to be in his embrace. She couldn't imagine anything would ever feel better. They stood that way for a long moment before Cade eased back and set her away from him. Megan wasn't sure what had gone wrong. Could she have imagined the heat in his eyes or the way his breath had hitched when she'd kissed him?

* * *

FUREVER YOURS:
Finding forever homes—and hearts!—
has never been so easy

Dear Reader,

The past can be a powerful force. If we aren't careful, things best left behind us will keep us from enjoying the present or from seeing the possibilities the future holds. Cade Battle, the hero in *The City Girl's Homecoming*, is a prisoner of his past. He's letting the hurt of a broken relationship blind him, leaving him unable to see what is right in front of his face—Megan Jennings, a woman with a heart of gold. Instead of opening his heart to the happiness that a relationship with Megan can bring, he holds on to the past with both hands.

Megan has loved and lost, leaving her a bit wary of giving her heart again. She's moved to Spring Forest in an attempt to make a break from the past. When she's asked to find homes for an elderly neighbor's sixteen cats and dogs, Megan can't say no. Cade's father volunteers to foster the animals on his family's farm until they can find their forever homes, so Megan and Cade are thrown together. Caring for the animals, they grow close. If they're willing to leave the past behind them and take a chance, they just might find the love they've longed for.

I love hearing from my readers, so feel free to visit my website, kathydouglassbooks.com, and drop me a line. While you're there, sign up for my newsletter. If you follow me on BookBub, you'll be informed whenever I have a new book coming out.

I hope you enjoy Megan and Cade's story.

Happy reading!

Kathy

The City Girl's Homecoming

—

Kathy Douglass

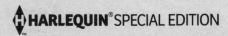
HARLEQUIN® SPECIAL EDITION

Special thanks and acknowledgment to Kathy Douglass for her contribution to the Furever Yours continuity.

Recycling programs
for this product may
not exist in your area.

ISBN-13: 978-1-335-57386-5

The City Girl's Homecoming

Copyright © 2019 by Harlequin Books S.A.

Printed in U.S.A.

Kathy Douglass came by her love of reading naturally—both of her parents were readers. She would finish one book and pick up another. Then she attended law school and traded romances for legal opinions.

After the birth of her two children, her love of reading turned into a love of writing. Kathy now spends her days writing the small-town contemporary novels she enjoys reading.

Books by Kathy Douglass

Harlequin Special Edition

Sweet Briar Sweethearts

How to Steal the Lawman's Heart
The Waitress's Secret
The Rancher and the City Girl
Winning Charlotte Back
The Rancher's Return

To Melissa, Teri, Stacy, Karen and Christy.
It was a pleasure!

As always, much love to my three personal heroes,
my husband and two sons.

Chapter One

Megan Jennings parked her midnight-blue Mercedes sedan on the edge of the driveway of the Whitaker sisters' house and stared in amazement. Could she actually be seeing what she thought she was seeing? Leaning forward, she peered through the windshield. She blinked several times but the image remained. No, she wasn't hallucinating. A man really was wrestling with the biggest pig she'd ever seen in her life. Judging by the sweat glistening on the man's muscular chest, the battle had been going on for some time. From the squealing and fighting the pig was doing, the match wasn't going to end any time soon.

The pig shoved the man against the side of the truck. The man grunted and temporarily lost his hold on the pig. Seeing an opportunity, the animal made a break for it. Cursing, the man threw himself on the pig, and the two rolled around on the grass.

Growing up in New York City, Megan had seen many strange sights in her twenty-eight years. In a few minutes spent walking around Times Square she could see everything from a naked cowboy to people dressed as cartoon characters. Over time, the sights had become humdrum and hadn't caused her to even take a second look. But this? This was something beyond even her imagination.

She'd moved to Spring Forest, North Carolina, from Manhattan a couple of months ago. She liked the small town and was adjusting to the slower pace and different lifestyle. And yet, in all that time, she'd never seen anything remotely like this. Or a man built quite so well. And after having lived in a city filled with models and actors whose livelihood was at least in part based upon their good looks, that was saying something.

Intrigued, she turned off the car and crept closer to the action. She didn't know much about pigs or the men who wrestled them, so she stepped cautiously, ready to return to the safety of her car if necessary. Her four-inch heels made walking on the gravel driveway a bit of an adventure, but she wouldn't have dreamed of wearing flats. Even though she now lived in a small town, she still retained some of her big-city habits. She still wore the suits she'd worn while working at a major New York law firm. The professional garments gave her the confidence that had been stripped from her after her family's unexpected deaths and the years spent in foster care.

Close up, the pig wrestler was something to behold.

Tall, with muscles that clearly came from years of hard work, and a face that could only be described as sexy, he could make a fortune as a model if he ever wanted a career change. Looking at what he was doing now—the enormous pig froze, then threw its entire body at the man—any job would be a step up. Of course, that was all contingent upon his surviving the encounter with the gigantic animal, something that was not assured at the moment.

The man's lips were moving, but he was speaking too quietly for her to hear what he was saying. Curiosity got the better of her and Megan came as close as she dared.

"Keep it up and you'll be roasting on a spit," the man threatened under his breath. His voice was deep, and despite the words he was muttering, quite sexy. The pig shoved against the man in response, drawing another grunt. "The sisters like me, so they'll totally believe me when I say you escaped. Meanwhile you'll be Sunday dinner and leftovers for the week."

The pig didn't seem to appreciate the comment and in response bucked and jerked, making the man hold on for dear life. It looked like he was riding the pig like a wild horse. Megan wouldn't have been surprised if he'd tossed his cowboy hat—which had somehow managed to stay on his head during the entire encounter—into the air and yelled *yee-haw!* Unable to contain herself, Megan giggled at the absurdity of it all.

Startled by the sound, the man looked up at her and temporarily lost his grip on the pig, who broke free and turned toward the man. The man jumped in front of a ramp leading to the back of the pickup truck. Megan's breath caught in her throat as the angered animal lowered its head and charged. A strangled cry broke through her lips as the pig drew within inches of the man's bare torso. At the last second the man stepped gracefully out of the way and the pig ran up the ramp and into the back of the truck. In the blink of an eye, the man removed the ramp and then slammed the tailgate shut.

Whew. Megan realized she'd begun to perspire and drew a couple of fingers across her damp brow, removing the moisture before the man could notice. Relief that the pig-wrestler was all right mingled with amusement at the spectacle, and she began to laugh. "Oh, my goodness. I have never in my life seen anything like that."

The pig-wrangling man glanced over his shoulder at her, a fierce glare twisting his handsome face. At his look, the laughter died in her throat and her smile melted away. Clearly he didn't find her delight amusing.

She started to apologize, then gave herself a mental shake, stopping just in time. She wasn't going to let the man make her feel guilty for finding humor in the situation. She'd let several foster families squash her natural joy, making her feel bad about showing any expression of happiness. It was as if they'd wanted her to be as miserable as possible. Some had gone out of their way to make her so.

Well, she was in control of her life now and she wasn't going to let anyone determine what she should feel or how she should react.

The man grabbed a plaid shirt from the bumper of the truck and used it to wipe his sweaty face and torso before shoving his arms into the sleeves. He buttoned the bottom four buttons and jerked on the fabric as if trying to remove the wrinkles. He wiped at a huge grass stain a couple of times before dropping his hand, apparently deciding there was no sense fighting a losing battle.

When it became obvious that the man wasn't going to introduce himself, she took a step in his direction, hand extended. Before she could reach him, the back door of the house opened and Bunny Whitaker, one of the women she'd come to see, came down the stairs. "Yoo-hoo. Did you get Little Piggy into the truck, Cade?"

Little Piggy? Megan shook her head at the name. That pig was anything but little.

"Yes, ma'am."

If only Bunny knew that her friend had threatened to take that Little Piggy to market, she wouldn't be smiling at him right now.

"He didn't give you any trouble, did he?"

"No, ma'am. Not even a little bit."

Megan felt her eyes widen at his falsehood. If that fight hadn't been trouble, she didn't know what was.

"That's because he's such a good boy, aren't you, Little Piggy?" Bunny leaned into the back of the truck and rubbed the pig, who snorted.

Bunny straightened. "I really appreciate you taking him in for us. We hate to part with him, but Birdie and I don't have the room to keep him. I know you'll give him a good home."

"Yes, ma'am."

Bunny looked up. When she noticed Megan, she smiled. "Hello. Is it time for our meeting already?"

"I'm a little bit early," Megan said, closing the distance between them. "I'm still trying to get used to small-town traffic. When I leave my office I still factor in time for traffic jams that have yet to materialize."

"We don't have many of those. Not unless geese are crossing the road or somebody's cows get out. And don't worry if you're a little bit late. People around here aren't ruled by the clock. When you tend animals, you understand that things beyond your control can happen." She dusted her hands on her denim skirt. "Have the two of you met?"

"No." Megan said.

Bunny smiled and waved for Cade to come closer. He dragged his feet as he walked over, clearly reluctant to join them. Since he'd smiled at Bunny, Megan decided she was the reason for his reticence.

Once he was near, Bunny put her arm around Megan's waist. "This is Megan Jennings. She's new to town. Pretty as she is on the outside, she's even prettier on the inside. She's the new lawyer that Daniel Sutton hired to help him."

Megan felt her face and the tips of her ears grow hot, but she managed a smile that she hoped hid her embarrassment. She hadn't known Bunny long, but she knew the sweet older woman wouldn't deliberately hurt or embarrass anyone. Still, looking at the expression on the man's face, it was clear he didn't find Megan's looks or anything else about her appealing.

"And this is Cade Battle," Bunny continued. "He's

a great friend of mine and Birdie's. He's part owner of Battle Lands Farm and one of the best people I know. If you ever need help with anything, Cade is the man you should call. He's completely trustworthy."

Megan noticed that Cade seemed embarrassed at Bunny's effusive praise and color crept beneath his light brown skin. Knowing she wasn't the only one who was ill at ease made Megan feel slightly better. She held out her hand. "Nice to meet you, Cade."

He wiped his hand on his shirt, then shook hers. His grip was firm, but not the too-tight handshake men often gave when trying to intimidate her. Of course, those men had been opposing counsel, who—if they were any good—would have known squeezing her fingers didn't scare her. It pissed her off.

Cade's palm was covered with calluses, no doubt a by-product of the hard work he did on a daily basis. "Nice to meet you, Ms. Jennings."

His voice was even sexier when he wasn't out of breath, and it sent shivers dancing down her spine. What was that about? She smiled. "It's Megan."

"Megan," he repeated, although he didn't return her smile.

"Well, good. Now you've each made a friend." Bunny beamed with satisfaction and turned her attention to Cade. "I came out here to let you know lunch is on the table. And Megan, you're more than welcome to join us. We have plenty."

Cade shook his head and backed up. "I won't be able to stay after all, Bunny."

"No? Why not?"

The deliberate way he didn't look in her direction gave Megan a sneaking suspicion. She wasn't the paranoid type, nor was she so conceited that she thought she was the driving force behind everyone's actions, but in this moment, based on his behavior, she believed she was the reason Cade didn't want to stay.

"I need to get going. There's a lot of work waiting for me. And getting Little Piggy settled may take longer than I had anticipated."

"Okay," Bunny looked crestfallen for a moment, but then she rallied. "At least let me give you a couple slices of cake."

"You don't have to do that," he said, but Bunny had already made her way up the stairs and into the house.

Neither Cade nor Megan spoke for a moment. She'd seen Cade around town a couple of times, but they'd never actually interacted with each other. Every time she'd gotten near him, he'd frowned at her like he was doing now. She'd heard that everyone had a twin somewhere in the world, so she'd comforted herself with the thought that he'd mistaken her for someone else. Someone who'd done him wrong. But now that Bunny had introduced them, it had to be clear to him that they'd never met. Yet he was still being incredibly unfriendly to her. He had to be the grumpiest man in town.

The silence stretched out, and neither of them made a move to break it. They were engaged in a strange battle of wills that Megan was determined to win. She didn't know why it mattered, but it was important that she let him know that she wasn't going to fall at his feet. Even as gorgeous as he was, she wasn't inclined to tolerate his unpleasant attitude.

"Here you go," Bunny said, coming back down the stairs. She handed him a paper bag and winked at him. "I added a couple of pieces of chicken just in case you get hungry on the way home."

"Thanks," he said. He smiled at the older woman. "I appreciate it."

Bunny stood on her tiptoes to give Cade a kiss on his cheek. He was so tall that he needed to lean over so she could reach him. Cade glanced at Megan, tipped his hat, then without a word got into his beat-up truck and drove away.

"Well now," Bunny said, taking Megan's arm. "I hope you're hungry. We have a feast."

Megan smiled, determinedly putting Cade Battle out of her mind. "I'm starved."

"Good," Bunny said as they climbed the stairs.

"Is there anything I can do to help?" Megan asked as they stepped into the kitchen. The aromas of fried chicken, fresh rolls, corn on the cob and pound cake greeted her as she stepped inside. The delicious smells reminded her of home. Or at least the home she'd had the first fourteen years of her life.

"No. I have it all under control," Birdie said stepping into the kitchen and going immediately to the stove. "Just have a seat and make yourself at home."

Megan pulled out a chair and sat down at the old oak table. Though the farmhouse was a hundred years old, the kitchen had clearly been renovated recently.

Megan first met the sisters a month ago when she'd

been assigned their case by her boss, Daniel Sutton. Birdie and Bunny had grown up in this house and had lived here all of their lives. Neither sister had ever married. They were different as night and day, but fit together like puzzle pieces. If there was an area where one was weak, the other was strong enough to compensate for it. Bernadette, who was called Birdie by everyone, was tall and thin and in great shape. She was a no-nonsense type who didn't tolerate fools, but underneath the gruff exterior, she was as generous and kind as could be. Gwendolyn, or Bunny, as she was affectionately called, was short and plump, with a heart of gold. She was a bit of a dreamer and a little too gullible and naive for Megan's comfort—thank goodness she had Birdie around to protect her—but she was always positive and encouraging. Megan liked them both very much.

"Cade still outside?" Birdie asked.

"No. He left. He had something to get back to," Bunny said.

Birdie only grunted. Megan hadn't known Birdie long enough to know what that sound meant, but apparently Bunny did.

"Exactly," Bunny replied. "I wrapped up some chicken and cake for him for the road."

Working in tandem, the sisters filled three plates to overflowing. Once they joined her at the table, Megan spoke. "I have some information for you."

"Not at lunch, dear. We never discuss business at meals. It's not good for digestion," Birdie said. "There's plenty of time for that later."

During her years of practice, Megan had had many

business lunches and dinners. And she'd always discussed business between bites. Most times business had been wrapped up before dessert. But then, that had been in New York, where everything moved at a much faster pace and no second could be wasted. Some days there had been barely enough time to breathe, much less eat a leisurely meal. But she was in Spring Forest now, and clearly, they did things differently here.

Since discussing business was forbidden, Megan picked up her corn on the cob and took a bite. It was delicious. Before moving to North Carolina, she'd shopped at farmers markets twice a week. She'd been impressed by the fruits and vegetables she'd purchased there, which tasted so much better than anything she'd bought at the store. But as good as that produce had tasted, it didn't compare to this. She'd never enjoyed such flavorful food before, and her taste buds smiled with pleasure.

"How are you adjusting to small-town life?" Birdie asked.

"It's different from New York, but I enjoy it. I like the peace and quiet and the sense of community. I like the way everyone pulls together to help those in need." Not that she hadn't experienced a sense of support and community in New York. She'd had two good friends she could count on. And they would continue to be her friends whether she lived in the same building or in an entirely different state. But she'd needed a change. She'd had to get away from Tim, her former fiancé, and his family.

She and Tim had met on their first day of law school and quickly fallen in love. They'd gotten engaged after they'd both passed the bar. His parents and his sisters had welcomed her into their family. She'd spent holidays and vacations with them, and they'd always made a big deal of her birthday. She'd been so sure that after all those years of bouncing from place to place in foster care, she'd finally found a family again.

Then she and Tim had broken up. Since the breakup had been friendly, Megan had believed she would remain friends with his family. She'd been wrong. She'd made excuses for them when they stopped returning her calls. But when her birthday came and went without acknowledgement, she'd realized they'd well and truly cut her from their lives.

She'd decided that the best way to deal with the painful situation was to make a clean break. On impulse, she'd written the names of the forty-nine other states on slips of paper and placed them in a hat. She'd pulled out North Carolina and had begun her job search there. Last month she'd been hired by Daniel Sutton, turning his one-man law firm into a one-man-and-one-woman firm. Sutton Law Office was very different from the five-hundred-lawyer firm where she'd worked before. It was a change, but not an unpleasant one.

While they ate, Megan and the Whitaker sisters chatted about Furever Paws, the animal rescue the sisters had founded on their property. The shelter, which was run mostly by volunteers, provided a necessary service in the community. Lost or unwanted pets were housed until new families could be found for them. The shelter held adoption fairs providing opportunities for the humans and animals to meet.

Once they'd eaten their cake and finished their sweet tea, Megan was able to steer the conversation to the reason she was here—their finances. She pulled a file from her leather bag and then looked from one sister to the other. Life had taught her that there was no such thing as sugarcoating bad news. Since Birdie and Bunny were going to be hurt, there was no use in beating around the bush.

"Well, ladies, I'm afraid what I have to say isn't good. Your brother Greg has been embezzling from you."

Bunny gasped and clasped her hands together against her chest.

Birdie shook her head. "Are you sure? I can't believe Gator would do that to us. Can you, Bunny?"

"No." Bunny's voice was barely over a whisper, but Megan heard the pain there.

Even though Megan had expected this response, her heart still ached for them. Bunny didn't want to believe anything bad about anyone, and Birdie had a blind spot when it came to her baby brother. Nothing he did would ever be wrong in her eyes. Even now, faced with evidence of his crimes, she still referred to him by the family's old, affectionate nickname.

Megan had the proof that he'd been stealing from them for years, but whether she could convince the sisters to do anything about it was anyone's guess. Still, she had to try. Bunny and Birdie were more than her clients. They were her friends. They were friends of the community. They cared about everyone and everyone cared about them.

"I have proof," she said, passing over copies of the

documents to each of them. Neither sister touched the stacks of papers. They barely looked at them. "This is the information from the forensic accountant I hired. I have time to go through everything now and answer any questions you have."

"I'm sure you do. We just aren't ready to think about any of this right now," Bunny said. "We need time to process what you've told us."

"I understand that, but it's important that we act sooner rather than later."

"We know, but we have other things to deal with right now and can't handle another."

"Like what?" Megan knew the news must be hard for them to grapple with, but putting off thinking about it wouldn't do them any favors—not when they were at risk of losing their home.

"Rebekah," Bunny replied immediately, and Birdie nodded.

"What about her?" Rebekah was the director of the animal shelter and one of Megan's new friends.

"There's something going on with her," Bunny replied. "She seems a little run-down and tired these days. I came upon her the other day and she looked positively ill."

"I saw her a few days ago and she looked fine to me," Megan said, hoping to end this discussion so she could get the sisters back on track.

"Do you think it could be stress from dealing with Grant?" Birdie asked as if Megan hadn't said a word. "That nephew of ours is such a perfectionist. He might be putting pressure on her."

"I wouldn't be surprised," Bunny said. "We should talk to him and make sure he knows how much we like Rebekah and how pleased we are with her work."

"That sounds like a good idea," Megan said. "But what are we going to do about your money? If Greg continues to steal from you, you'll be in big trouble. It's possible that you could lose everything, including your home, the rest of your land and the animal rescue."

At that bit of grim news, the sisters stopped talking about Rebekah and Grant and gave her their full attention. Birdie looked at her sister and then back at Megan. "Go on."

"I'd like to set up a trust that would protect your property and money that your brother currently doesn't control. Once we gain control of the rest, we'll be able to protect that, as well. And if neither of you is interested or feels qualified to act as trustee, I'll hire one for you."

The sisters shared a long look. "That would be all right," Birdie said finally.

"Great. I'll take care of that right away. Now, the second thing we need to discuss is whether or not you want to bring criminal charges against Greg."

"I don't know. I can't imagine putting my baby brother in jail," Birdie said.

"Your baby brother is robbing you blind," Megan pointed out. "If we hadn't caught him in time, you could have ended up on the street."

"Still...we need time to think about that."

"Good enough." At least she'd gotten them to take the first steps to protect themselves in the future. "Take your time and consider what I've told you. In the meantime, I'll get busy setting up the trust. I'll make sure that your brother doesn't have the ability to make financial decisions for you any longer. Your assets will be protected, although I can't promise we'll be able to get any of your money back. No doubt it's already gone."

"Okay." Birdie picked up the documents Megan had given to them and tried to hand them back.

"Those are your copies," Megan said. "I have my own. Read them over at your leisure. If you have any questions, I'm always available to answer them."

"Oh, there's no need for that, dear," Bunny said. "We trust you. It's good to know we're in such good hands."

Megan didn't bother to tell the older woman that it was that kind of blind trust that had landed them in the mess they were in. At her age, she wasn't likely to change. But since Megan was trustworthy and her boss Daniel was as well, she knew the sisters truly were in good hands. No one else would be able to harm them anymore.

Megan stood and grabbed her briefcase.

"Don't tell me you need to leave right now," Bunny said.

"I'm afraid so. Thanks again for lunch. It was wonderful." Megan walked beside the sisters to the front door. Before Megan stepped onto the shady porch, Bunny gave her a hug. Surprised, Megan froze. It had been a while since she'd been the recipient of such open affection. Pushing down unexpected emotions, she returned the hug, then walked to her car. As she drove away, she hoped the sisters would take her advice and bring criminal charges against their brother. Family was a precious thing, and anyone who took advantage of their siblings deserved to be punished.

As she headed for her office, her thoughts drifted back to Cade Battle. He was probably the best-looking man she'd ever seen, and undoubtedly the grumpiest. Still, he'd been kind to Bunny so she knew he couldn't be all bad. Not that it mattered. He clearly didn't like her.

And she couldn't help wonder why it bothered her so much that he didn't.

Chapter Two

As Cade turned from the driveway onto the road, his stomach growled in protest. He'd looked forward to lunch with the Whitaker sisters all morning. Birdie and Bunny were fabulous cooks and baked the absolute best desserts. While he'd been knocked around as he fought to get the pig into his truck, it had been the thought of the delicious meal waiting for him that had kept him going. And then Ms. Susie Sunshine in her power suit had come along and ruined it all.

Cade had seen her around town a few times over the past month. Who could miss her? Tall, with a curvy body and a stunning face, she was the most beautiful woman he'd ever seen in his life. Their eyes had met and locked on one of those occasions and his mouth had gone dry. He'd ignored the reaction. It had only taken one look at her impeccable makeup, gorgeous hair, perfectly manicured nails and stylish clothes to instantly know the type of woman she was. He'd once been in love with her type. He'd been left heartbroken by her type. He needed to avoid her type.

She had city girl written all over her. There wasn't the slightest doubt in his mind that she'd moved to Spring Forest because she was running from something. Perhaps she thought that a change of scenery would fix whatever was wrong with her life. But once she'd recovered from her broken heart or lost job or whatever it was that had sent her here, she'd hightail it out of North Carolina so fast she'd leave a trail of smoke behind her.

Just look at her clothes. She dressed as if she was still living in the city. He knew she was a lawyer, but Daniel Sutton was, too, and he didn't walk around wearing three-piece suits. No, he dressed like he was a member of the community, not someone who was passing through on the way to someplace better.

Cade had made the mistake of believing his former fiancée could be happy living a quiet life on the Battle Lands Farm. Deadra had sworn that she loved him and that sharing her life with him was all she wanted. Then she'd left him for a slick Chicago lawyer and hadn't looked back. He'd been fooled once by a pretty city woman. He wouldn't make that mistake again.

Despite knowing the danger she presented to his emotional well-being, there was something about Megan Jennings that appealed to him. He'd heard her gasp when Little Piggy had charged him, and knew it was because she'd been afraid for him. Though clearly her fear was rooted in her concern for a fellow human and not him specifically, her reaction had warmed his heart. It didn't change the fact that she was a city girl. And it certainly didn't mean he would let down his guard with her. Still, it was proof that a caring heart beat beneath that designer suit.

Frowning, Cade turned on the radio, hoping the music would erase all thoughts of Megan and the sound of her laughter from his mind. It didn't work. Despite the singer's voice and the sound of the drums and bass, he could still hear Megan's sexy alto voice. Just hearing her say his name had been enough to set his imagination racing in the wrong direction. And he could still picture her sparkling eyes. But none of that mattered. He didn't have time for a woman, even if he met one who would be happy living here. He had plans.

Cade switched off the radio and drove the rest of the way home in silence. When he reached the farm, he signaled and turned into the driveway beneath the iron sign announcing the Battle Lands Farm. Rather than stopping at the front of the house, he continued to the back to where the barns were located. The pig, which had been relatively quiet, suddenly began to snort and move around as much as it could in the truck bed.

The back door of his father's house opened and he stepped outside. Although his dad was in his midfifties, he was still strong as an ox. With his father's help, it would be a lot easier to get the pig out of the truck than it had been to get it in.

"So, this is our new guest," his dad said, with a smile. Reginald Battle took being a good neighbor to new heights. If there was someone he could help, he did without hesitation. If he couldn't help, he didn't rest until he found someone who could. Never once in his life had Cade seen his father reject anyone's request for assistance. While their farm wasn't an animal rescue, they constantly took in animals that the Whitaker sisters were unable to accommodate. The pig was just the latest in a string of goats, chickens and geese that had come to reside on their farm. This was their first pig. And given how difficult it was to get it into the truck, Cade hoped it would be the last.

"This is him." Cade shook his head and grinned. "Bunny called him Little Piggy."

Reginald roared at the name. "She didn't think that one through."

"Not at all. Anyway, I want to get this pig settled in the barn. This little trip has set me behind on the work I planned to do for the day."

"Then let's get this one into his new home."

Cade backed the truck up to the barn, and then he put the ramp in place. He and Reginald exchanged looks and at his father's nod, Cade lowered the tailgate. The pig wasted no time in going from the bed of the truck into the barn. Once they got the pig inside, Cade heaved a sigh of relief. His father had already filled the feeding troughs with food and water. Reginald always claimed being a good neighbor didn't cost a thing, but Cade knew that wasn't true. In this case, it cost valuable time on top of maintenance costs, such as extra feed. Battle Lands Farm was profitable and could easily absorb the cost. Cade, on the other hand, got the same twenty-four hours as everyone else, so he would have to work faster and harder to make up for lost time.

"So, how are your plans going?"

"Not bad." Cade was developing a farm-to-table business. He'd convinced his father to go organic several years ago, believing it was better for their customers as well as the environment. The business was what he should be focusing on instead of how sweet Megan Jennings smelled. "I've just finalized the marketing plan and I've determined how much produce I'll have available for this year's trial. I'm also working on a delivery schedule. But, none of this will make a bit of difference if I don't have any customers. Then I'll end up selling everything to grocery stores again."

"I know you don't like doing that."

"No." Cade worked hard to produce the best fruits and vegetables. He wanted the people who ate that food to get the best flavor and the maximum amount of nutrients. That meant dining on the food within a day or two of it being harvested, not after weeks. In order to accomplish that, he needed to have local clients in the restaurant business who shared his vision. He would continue to provide produce at the farmer's market that was held at the Granary's parking lot from late spring to early fall. But he wanted to move the business in this other direction, as well. Until he had enough clients for his farm-to-table produce, he would continue to supply grocery chains.

"It'll work out. I'm sure of that. Once you put your mind to something, Cade, you always find a way to make it happen. You'll figure this out, too."

Cade appreciated his father's support. Of course, it

would be easier to pull this off if his mind was focused on his plan and not the very beautiful and oh-so-wrong for him Megan Jennings.

When Megan was finished with her meeting at Whitaker Acres, she returned to her office. The drive had enabled her to clear her mind. There was something so peaceful about driving on roads that weren't so congested that traveling three miles took nearly half an hour. The scenic countryside was an extra added bonus.

She loved this little town. Only about twenty miles from downtown Raleigh, it was an easy commute to the state capital. And though it had the requisite chain stores, the town possessed a charm and personality all its own. The downtown had many small businesses that made Spring Forest unique. Snap Pop Candy Shop, Whole Bean Coffee, and Mimzi's Ice Cream, all within walking distance of her office, had been major selling points in her decision to take the job. There was something about the small town that gave her a sense of home. It felt familiar even though she'd never been here before.

She parked her car at the back of the converted craftsman house that served as the Sutton Law Office building and went inside.

Emma Alvarez, the office manager and Daniel's fiancée was at her desk when Megan arrived. She looked up. "How did it go with Bunny and Birdie?"

"Only time will tell. Right now they're in denial. Birdie can't believe that Gator would steal from them. I tried to show them the proof we have, but they wouldn't even look at it. I left copies with them. Hopefully they'll read the files and decide to press charges."

Emma patted Megan's hand. "You've done all you can. That's all you can expect of yourself."

"I know." Megan was silent for a moment.

"What else happened?"

Although they hadn't known each other long, Emma was pretty attuned to Megan. There was no sense trying to deceive her. "I met the grumpiest man in town."

"Who?"

"Cade Battle. I think he'd intended to stay for lunch until I got an invitation. Then he suddenly didn't have time. He was just this side of rude."

"Rude? To you? Why?"

Megan shrugged. "I have no idea."

"As good as the sisters cook, missing lunch is no more than he deserved."

"True." Emma's diamond solitaire sparkled on her left ring finger, catching Megan's eye. "It's getting close to the big day."

Emma nodded. "I can hardly wait."

"I bet." Megan knew firsthand the excitement that came with planning a wedding. And she knew the disappointment that came when the wedding was called off and the couple didn't become a family. She really hoped Emma and Daniel managed to pull it off. They were good people and deserved to be happy.

Emma glanced at the clock and shut down her computer. "I need to get going. It's time for me to pick up the girls."

Emma had initially been hired by Daniel as a nanny

for his three daughters. Once he realized how organized she was, he'd asked her to become his temporary office manager, working from 8 a.m. until 2 p.m. Somewhere in there, they'd fallen in love. Emma kept the same hours so she could be available for her soon-to-be stepdaughters.

"See you tomorrow," Megan said, walking to her office at the back of the building. The office was so different from the one she'd had at her New York firm. That one had been outfitted with expensive furniture. Original artwork had hung on the walls. This one was simply decorated and had a homey feel to it. While her New York office had been designed to impress clients, this office was designed to make her clients feel comfortable.

Megan updated her case files to reflect her meeting with the sisters and then put a reminder on her calendar to follow up with them. That simple task had her once more thinking about Cade Battle and the way he looked with his shirt off. He was definitely well built. There was something about him that appealed to her on a basic level. She quickly slammed the door on that thought reminding herself that he didn't like her. After returning calls to other clients, she turned off her computer and headed for the Main Street Grille.

It was only a couple of blocks from the office, so she decided to walk and return for her car after she'd gotten her order.

As expected, the Grille was doing brisk business. The food, burgers and sandwiches for lunch with typical pub offerings added to the dinner menu was anything but typical. The burgers were juicy and flavorful. The corned beef on a Kaiser roll and pastrami on rye tasted as good as the sandwiches she'd bought at her favorite deli in New York.

She looked around. The tables and booths were filled with families enjoying a night out together and a yearning grew within her. Two children near her laughed, the sound mingling with boisterous conversation. Someone bumped into her and she looked around.

"Sorry," a man's voice said.

Megan looked up and into Cade's face and her silly heart skipped a beat. His eyes swept over her and her skin began to tingle as if he'd actually touched her. She'd never had such a strong reaction to a man and the intensity of the feeling surprised her.

"I didn't see you standing there," Cade said. A hint of something she didn't recognize flashed in his eyes for a moment only to be replaced by coolness and indifference. He stepped away from her. Disappointment settled in her stomach.

"Don't worry about it," she said. "It's crowded in here."

He nodded then looked around as if searching for someone. Clearly he was uninclined to continue the conversation.

"Do you come here a lot?" Megan asked. It seemed foolish to be standing there and not talk. After all, they might not be friends, but they weren't strangers any longer.

"Often enough."

That was vague. What, did he think she would stalk

him by hanging around here on a regular basis hoping to see him? That wasn't likely. Megan refused to chase a man, no matter how handsome he was or how much faster her heart beat when he was around.

Although Megan liked the food, she didn't dine here often. She rented a house in the historic part of town about a twenty-minute walk from the office. Although small, the house had a very nice kitchen. Most days she cooked dinner for herself and her elderly neighbor, Mrs. Crockett. The older woman had mentioned having a hankering for a steak and fries from the Grille, so Megan had decided to grab the food here today. She considered letting Cade know he was safe from her, but decided against it. Instead she marched to the counter and gave her to go order. Once placed, she stood by the front window and waited for it, refusing to look at him again. The seconds seemed to crawl until her order was ready. When her name was called, she ran to the counter and grabbed the brown bag and headed home.

Cade watched as Megan Jennings took her bag and left. Though he told himself not to stare, he couldn't keep his eyes from focusing on her curvy backside as she strode from the restaurant. After their brief encounter, she hadn't looked in his direction once, choosing to look out the window instead. Not that he wanted her attention. He didn't.

The last thing he wanted was to have Megan Jennings anywhere near his life. She was a city woman through and through and he didn't need that kind of trouble. When he decided to have a relationship again, it was going to be with a nice country girl. Someone who loved the farm life as much as he did. So why was his mind suddenly filled with thoughts of Megan?

"Who's the girl?"

"Nobody," Cade said, turning to his brother. Chase must have arrived while Cade had been distracted by Megan. "Let's grab a table."

"It didn't look like nobody," Chase said as he slid into the booth.

"Nobody important," Cade clarified.

Chase laughed. "Really?"

"Yes. I only met her today. So whatever you're thinking, forget about it."

"What I was thinking is that it looks to me like a city girl has gotten your attention. Not that I have a problem with that."

"You're not the one who was burned."

"True. But from the way you were staring, it doesn't look as if you've learned your lesson."

Cade didn't bother telling his brother just how wrong he was. Cade had learned his lesson good and well. He'd never let a girl like Megan near his heart again. "Forget about her. I'm sure you didn't come all the way to Spring Forest to harass me. Let's eat."

Megan arrived at home and changed out of her work clothes into a pair of green cotton shorts and a coordinating floral top. Green had been her mother's favorite color and Megan wore something in that color every day to honor her mother's memory. Some days Megan missed her family so much her heart actually ached. Wearing green helped her feel closer to her mother.

Megan grabbed the bag containing dinner then walked across the street to her neighbor's house. Mrs. Crockett had been widowed many years ago and had never remarried. Most people believed the elderly woman was weird or crazy, and consequently no one ever visited her.

The day Megan moved into her house, she'd witnessed the woman holding a conversation with one of her sixteen cats and dogs. Megan could have turned her back on the other woman like everyone else in town had chosen to do, but she hadn't. She recognized loneliness when she saw it. So instead, she'd approached the woman and introduced herself. Mrs. Crockett had smiled broadly and introduced each of the animals by name. Then she'd invited Megan in for a glass of sweet tea. In no time flat they'd become fast friends, and Megan brought her dinner each night.

Megan knocked on the door. Within seconds it opened.

"Oh, is that dinner? You know you don't have to cook for me all the time."

Megan smiled at the protest. Mrs. Crockett only received a pittance from Social Security and her late husband's pension. Unfortunately her limited income wasn't sufficient to cover care for the animals, pay rent and buy sufficient groceries for herself. Mrs. Crockett had chosen to prioritize the first and frequently didn't have food. She also hadn't paid her rent in quite a while and was only days away from being evicted. Daniel and

Megan had done all they could to help, but had run out of options. No matter how often they'd advised her of the consequences of her choices, Mrs. Crockett insisted on taking care of the animals regardless of the cost to herself. As a result, she was about to lose her home.

"It's just as easy to cook for two as for one. But today I picked up dinner at the Grille. I got that steak you said you wanted."

"You can't tell me you want to spend your Friday evening with an old woman. Surely the men in town must be beating down your door to get you to go out with them."

"You live across the street from me," Megan pointed out with a smile as she put the carryout containers onto the table. "Have you seen any men, young or otherwise, knocking on my door?"

Mrs. Crockett tsked as she poured sweet tea into crystal glasses. The table had been set with delicate china and a vase of fresh flowers that came from her garden. Embroidered napkins matched the lacy tablecloth. The care her neighbor took to make the table look so nice illustrated how much she looked forward to their meals.

"I don't know what's wrong with the young men in this town. In my day, men knew how to come courting. My Harvey was such a charmer." Mrs. Crockett glanced at the picture of her late husband that sat in a place of honor on the upright piano. Though the photograph had faded with time, Megan could still make out the young man's proud smile. "He never once showed up on my doorstep empty-handed. He always brought flowers or candy or some trinket he knew I would like. Men these days don't have a clue. Or manners. They don't even hold the door for you. And sometimes they only want what you young people refer to as a booty call."

Megan had just taken a bite of her pastrami sandwich and nearly choked at the older woman's comment. She took a swallow of her tea. "Where did you hear that phrase?"

Mrs. Crockett laughed. "I may be an old woman, but I do have a television and radio. Not to mention the internet. I know all about what's going on in this crazy world."

"Apparently," Megan said with a laugh.

"Now, if my sweet boy Willie was still alive, he could show you the way a young man should behave."

Willie had been Mrs. Crockett's only child. He'd followed in his father's footsteps and joined the Army. Sadly he'd died in an unfortunate training accident while in his twenties. Of course had Willie lived, he would be old enough to be Megan's father. Not that she would ever point that out. Megan knew Willie would forever be twenty-six in Mrs. Crockett's memory as well as in her heart.

"I'm sure you raised him right."

"That I did." Mrs. Crockett focused on her meal for a few minutes before speaking again. "Surely you must have met someone in the time you've been here. Someone who could help you forget the ex-boyfriend you left behind in New York."

Megan immediately pictured Cade Battle in all his shirtless glory, then just as quickly dismissed him. She might not know everything about men, but she could tell when one wasn't interested in her. And Cade Battle definitely fit into that category. Their encounter at the Grille this evening had emphasized that. Not only that, he actually appeared to dislike her, although she couldn't for the life of her imagine why. They'd never even met before today. "Nope. Not a one."

"That's a shame. I don't know what's wrong with men your age."

Megan heard the disappointment in the older woman's voice. "Well, I haven't been in town long. I'm sure I'll meet someone soon."

That seemed to pacify Mrs. Crockett, and their conversation drifted to other topics. Once they'd finished eating, they carried their plates to the kitchen and washed them. A delicious-smelling peach cobbler was cooling on the counter. Mrs. Crockett placed heaping helpings into etched glass bowls and added a scoop of vanilla ice cream. As usual, they ate their dessert at the kitchen table. The night was pleasant, and the window was open, letting in the sweet breeze. Megan was going to miss sharing these companionable nights with her neighbor.

"I've talked to your grandniece, Grace," Megan said. She'd avoided the conversation while they'd eaten the main course, but knew she had to bring it up.

Mrs. Crockett lifted her eyebrow but didn't reply. Instead she scraped her spoon around the inside of her bowl.

"I know you don't want to move in with her family and you won't have to. Grace has found a wonderful senior living home. She visited the facility and liked it. Best of all, it's only twenty minutes away from her house, so she and her children will be able to visit you regularly. And you'll be able to visit her."

"I appreciate all that you and Daniel are trying to do for me," Mrs. Crockett said, speaking slowly.

"But?"

"How can I possibly leave my babies? They need me. I can't just abandon them to fend for themselves again. If I can't stay in this house, then fine. I'll just have to think of something else."

"There is nothing else," Megan said gently. She'd tried every legal maneuver she could think of, pushing the envelope as she stretched her creativity. Nothing worked. Mrs. Crockett was going to be evicted.

One of the cats rubbed against Mrs. Crockett's leg. She picked him up and rubbed her nose into his fur. "So you just expect me to turn my back on them and forget they exist? I can't."

When other people looked at Mrs. Crockett they saw a crazy cat and dog woman. Megan saw more than that. She saw a woman with a kind heart and a lot of love to give. People judged her because she chose to give that love to stray animals. Megan knew the reason why she did that. Mrs. Crockett had once told Megan that animals didn't join the military and break their mother's heart. Mrs. Crockett couldn't risk loving people again. That didn't mean people couldn't love her.

"I've been thinking about that and I believe I have a solution."

"Let's hear it." Though Mrs. Crockett might have been trying to sound cool, Megan heard the hope and excitement in her voice.

"The Whitaker sisters run the Furever Paws Animal Rescue on their property. We can take the animals there."

"Bunny and Birdie?"

Megan nodded.

"They've always been nice girls."

The Whitaker sisters were in their sixties and hadn't been girls in nearly half a century. But then Mrs. Crockett was ninety years old, so even at their advanced age, they still seemed like girls to her.

"Then you know they'll take good care of your animals."

"I'm sure the shelter is a good place, but I want more than that for my babies. I want them to have good homes where they'll be loved."

"The shelter tries to find good homes for the animals."

"Can you promise they'll find a home for mine?"

"I don't think they'll be able to keep them all together," Megan said honestly.

"No, I don't suppose they will."

"But I'll make sure they each find a good family. I promise you that."

Mrs. Crockett heaved a heavy sigh, then looked around her kitchen. "So many memories. I look around this house and there are memories everywhere. I moved in here after my Harvey died. I raised my boy here. I'm going to miss this place."

"I know. And if there was a legal way you could stay here, I would be in court arguing it. But there isn't."

"I know. I appreciate all that you've done for me."

"The new place your grandniece found sounds nice. You'll have a private room. The room is big enough for you to have a small sitting area, so you'll be able to take some of your own furniture. It won't be the same as living here, but it's still something. And of course you'll carry your memories inside you."

"You'll find good homes for all of them? No matter how long it takes?"

Megan drew her finger across her chest. "I cross my heart."

"All right then, I'll go."

Thank goodness. Megan stood. "I'll be back tomorrow morning to help you pack."

Mrs. Crockett stood, as well. When they reached the front door, she gave Megan a hug. "You're a good girl, Megan. I hope you find a family soon, too."

Megan nodded. After fourteen years of searching and not finding one, she knew it wasn't going to be nearly as easy as finding families for the animals.

Chapter Three

As Megan turned onto the gravel parking lot of Furever Paws Animal Rescue, her eyes drifted down the road toward Whitaker Acres. She couldn't help but remember yesterday, and her eyes shot to the place where she'd seen Cade Battle wrestling with the giant pig. She wouldn't mind getting another view of Cade's sculpted, shirtless torso. Unfortunately he was nowhere in sight.

The animal shelter was in a sturdy, sunny-yellow one-story building with a silhouette of a cat and a dog inside a heart on the front. The logo was clearly designed to assure everyone who brought in strays or pets they could no longer care for that those animals would be well loved.

Megan stepped inside and was immediately greeted by a smiling volunteer who was manning the front desk.

"Hi. I'm Megan Jennings. I was hoping to see Rebekah, if she's not too busy at the moment?"

"Let me check for you," the cheery woman said. She picked up a phone and spoke briefly then hung up. "Go on back. Hers is the office on the left."

Megan thanked the woman and walked to the office. Rebekah was sitting at her desk and waved for Megan to come in. The other woman looked green around the gills, and Megan remembered the Whitaker sisters' concern for her health. Maybe they were right to be worried.

"Are you okay?" Megan asked as she sat down in the chair in front of Rebekah's desk.

Rebekah lifted a water bottle to her mouth and took a sip. Her hand shook. "I'm fine."

Megan had only lived in town a couple of months, so although she and Rebekah were friendly, Megan didn't know the other woman well enough to press for a deeper answer. Foster care had taught her not to force herself into spaces where she hadn't been invited. Since Rebekah didn't seem inclined to confide in her, Megan got down to business. "Good. I wanted to talk to you a bit about the process for bringing animals into the shelter."

Rebekah blinked as if surprised by the change in subject and then smiled. "Of course. All of the animals have to be examined by a veterinarian before they're allowed to stay here. We need to make sure they have had all of their vaccinations. We also spay or neuter them if that's necessary. Until then, they're quarantined. We have to make sure they don't have communicable diseases. Once we're sure that they're healthy, they're either fostered or taken into the shelter. Do you have an animal that you want to bring in?"

"No. My neighbor is moving and won't be able to take her pets with her."

"Pets as in plural? How many are we talking about?"

"Sixteen. Eight dogs and eight cats."

Rebekah leaned back in her chair and shook her head. "I'm sorry. We can't accommodate that many animals right now. Right now we don't have room for even one."

Megan sighed, disheartened. "I promised that I would help her find homes for her animals. I can't go back on my word. And even though she's on the verge of being evicted, she won't move unless she knows her pets are going to be taken care of. I'll pay for the examinations and vaccinations if that makes a difference."

"It doesn't. The cost isn't the problem. Our volunteer vet, Doc J, is a good friend of Birdie and Bunny, so he does all of the examinations for free. The problem is the lack of space. We just don't have room for that many animals right now."

"I understand." Megan stood.

"I'm sorry we can't help," Rebekah said, standing as well. At least Rebekah no longer looked pale.

"So am I." As Megan left the sanctuary, her mind whirled. There had to be a solution. She couldn't tell Mrs. Crockett that her pets would be homeless. Megan wished she could take them in herself, but it wasn't practical. Unlike Mrs. Crockett, she didn't have a fenced-in backyard, so she couldn't let the animals outside on their own. They might wander off and get lost, or worse, hit by a car. Leaving them indoors wouldn't work either, since Megan worked and the animals would be cooped up inside most days. That wouldn't be fair to the cats and dogs. Still, there had to be a solution.

She was opening her car door when she heard Birdie calling to her. Smiling, Megan closed the door and waited for the older woman to reach her. Megan wondered if Birdie and her sister had reached a decision about whether to prosecute their brother. Personally Megan hoped they'd throw the book at him, but it wasn't up to her.

"Hello," Birdie said as she drew near. "What brings you out here on this lovely Saturday?"

"I was hoping that I could drop off a few animals at the shelter. Unfortunately there isn't enough room for them."

"No? How many are you talking about?"

"Sixteen. They're Mrs. Crockett's. She's moving and needs to find a home for them."

"Hmm." Birdie tapped her chin and a bit of mischief flickered in her eyes, then disappeared so quickly Megan might have imagined it. "I might know someone who can help you."

"Really? That would be great." Because there was no way she was telling Mrs. Crockett that her "babies" weren't going to be taken care of after all.

"Yes. The sanctuary often gets too many animals that we can't take care of. When that happens, we call on a couple of good friends of ours with an enormous farm and they take them in. You met the son the other day. I'm sure Reginald and Cade will be more than happy to house the animals while we work to find homes for them."

Megan's heart skipped at Cade's name. What was that about? It was one thing to appreciate a good-looking man. Any woman with eyes would do that. It was another thing entirely to start to feel something—anything—like interest or attraction for a man who'd made it abundantly clear not once but twice that he didn't like her. The wise thing to do was avoid Cade at all costs. But she had to think about the animals.

"Do you think they'll be willing? It's one thing to take in a pig, which is actually a farm animal, and another to take on sixteen cats and dogs. Some of them don't even get along."

"Cade and Reginald are sweethearts. They haven't let me down once. They understand what it means to be a good neighbor."

Megan bit her tongue. Cade might know what it meant to be a good neighbor, but you couldn't tell it by the way he'd treated her. Or maybe he didn't think of her as his neighbor. Maybe he was one of those people who looked at anyone who wasn't born locally as an outsider.

Not that she disagreed with that description. She was an outsider and had been since she was fourteen and her entire family had been wiped out. The four years she'd spent in foster homes had taught her that no matter how hard you tried, you couldn't squeeze yourself into a unit that didn't want to include you. But this wasn't about her. This was about the animals, so she needed to put her doubts aside. "If you're sure."

"I'm positive. If you want, I'll give you directions to Battle Lands Farm."

"Thank you." Megan scribbled the information in the

notepad she always kept with her. She'd drop by the farm after work on Monday. She'd always preferred to have important conversations in person. She thought about asking Birdie if she and Bunny had reached a decision about their brother, then decided against it. This visit didn't have anything to do with that case. In fact, had Birdie not approached her, they wouldn't have spoken today. Megan didn't want Birdie to feel pressured. "See you soon."

Birdie waved as she walked away. Megan watched until the older woman stepped inside the building, and then she got in her car and drove away. It looked like she had a place to take the animals after all. That is, if the grumpy pig-wrestling farmer agreed.

Cade was closing the barn door when he heard a car motor, and he turned around. He recognized the luxury sedan as belonging to Megan Jennings. The blood began to pulse in his veins as her image flashed in his mind. Despite knowing that she wasn't right for him, he couldn't help noticing how beautiful she was. Tall and curvaceous, she was physically everything that appealed to him. Too bad everything else about her was absolutely wrong. Yet as he stood and waited for her car to reach him, he couldn't slow the pounding of his heart.

He watched as she parked and then got out of her car. As one high heel emerged from the vehicle, he shook his head. Who wore four-inch pumps on a working farm? A woman who didn't belong, that's who. He had to give her credit, though. She walked in them easily, her sexy hips swaying with each step, and he had to force his eyes to her face.

There was only one word that could describe her face and that was breathtaking. It wasn't a word that he used often, but it was the only one that adequately defined the difficulty he had breathing when looking at her. She really did take his breath away.

When his eyes met hers, his rebellious heart skipped a beat. He crossed his arms over his chest in an unfriendly pose as if warning his heart that being attracted to Megan was unacceptable.

"What can I do for you, Ms. Jennings?" he said as soon as she was close enough to hear him. The light in her eyes dimmed and he felt a twinge of guilt at his cool tone. She hadn't hurt him.

"It's Megan. And I've come to ask a favor."

"A favor?"

"That's right."

"What is it you think I can do for you?" he asked when she didn't elaborate.

"It's not actually for me. I'm here on behalf of my neighbor, Mrs. Crockett. She's moving and I told her that I would find homes for her cats and dogs. I thought they might be able to take them at Furever Paws, but they can't. Birdie suggested that you might house the animals temporarily until permanent homes can be found for them."

"No way. This is a working farm, not an animal shelter. You wasted your time coming here." He turned to walk away.

"It wouldn't be for long," she said, grabbing his arm.

His skin burned where her slender fingers made contact and he gritted his teeth. He was not falling for another city girl. He might not be the smartest man in the world, but surely he had enough sense not to make the same mistake again. So why didn't his body get the message?

He untangled her fingers from his arm and took a step back. "I don't have the time to look after a bunch of pets."

He heard the back door open and cursed under his breath. His father walked down the stairs and joined them, giving Megan a wide smile. "Why hello, young lady. I'm Reginald Battle, Cade's dad. I don't think we've met."

Megan smiled in return and held out her hand. Her nails were perfectly manicured and painted a bright pink. Cade wanted to kick himself for noticing. "Hello, sir. It's nice to meet you. I'm Megan Jennings. I haven't lived in Spring Forest very long. Just a couple of months."

"You don't say. Well, the town is definitely more beautiful with you around."

Cade scowled, annoyed by his father's comment.

Megan giggled, and her light brown skin turned an attractive shade of pink. "Thank you."

"So what brings you out to our farm? You and Cade don't have a date, do you?" Reginald sounded a bit too hopeful for Cade's liking. Surely his father didn't think Cade should start dating again so soon.

"No." If she thought the question was outrageous, she didn't show it. "I was actually here to ask a favor of your son. Sadly he isn't able to help me."

"What kind of favor?" Reginald asked, and Cade

mentally groaned. He already knew what was about to happen.

"My neighbor is moving into a senior center and I'm looking for someone to foster her pets until I can find good homes for them."

"Did you try Furever Paws? That's what they do."

"They don't have the space to handle Mrs. Crockett's animals."

Reginald rubbed his chin thoughtfully. "How many animals are you talking about?"

Megan blew out a breath. "Sixteen. Eight cats and eight dogs."

Reginald looked around the farm, and Cade knew what he was seeing. Although most of the acreage was dedicated to growing their organic produce or allowing space for their free-range chickens and grass-fed cows to wander, the ten acres immediately surrounding the house had no such purpose. It was simply grass and trees with a good-sized vegetable garden. There was plenty of space for dogs and cats to roam and play. The old barn could easily house the animals.

"We have plenty of room here," Reginald said. "The dogs can run around to their hearts' content and the cats can do whatever it is that cats do. And if you are worried about the dogs getting out, the corral fence can easily be modified to create a dog run."

Megan glanced back and forth between him and his father without speaking. He waited for her to pounce on Reginald's offer, but she didn't. Perhaps she didn't want to cause conflict between him and his father.

"I don't have time to take care of them, Dad."

Reginald clapped a hand on Cade's shoulder. "We always have time to help friends. This Mrs. Crockett needs help with her pets, and since we're in a position to provide it, don't you think we should? After all, we've benefitted from kind neighbors a time or two."

Cade sighed. His dad was right. A year ago Cade's mother had been ill with breast cancer. In the weeks before she'd succumbed to her illness, friends and neighbors had helped the family in every way imaginable. They'd brought food for every meal and kept house. They'd sat with Rose when she'd been up for company. They'd helped care for the animals and see to the other farm tasks, to free Cade and his father to stay at her bedside. They'd just been there.

"Okay. The animals can stay," Cade said reluctantly. He tried not to notice the way that Megan's face lit up as she smiled happily.

"Thank you so much. I can't tell you how much I appreciate this. Of course I'll buy all of the food and litter, so it won't cost you anything but space."

"That's not necessary," Cade said. "Food for sixteen and litter for eight will add up to a pretty penny. We can absorb the cost more easily than you can."

"Wow. Are you sure?" Now she looked from him to his dad.

"Of course," Reginald said. "Friends help each other, which is something you obviously know since you're helping Mrs. Crockett. And now that we've met, you can count us among your friends, Megan."

The smile Megan gave Cade's father could only be described as wistful, and despite telling himself he didn't care, Cade wondered about the emotion behind that expression.

"Thank you," she said quietly.

Reginald nodded and looked at Cade. "I came out here to let you know dinner's ready, Cade. And I made plenty, so Megan, you're more than welcome to join us."

"Thank you for the offer, but I have other plans."

Cade fought back a strange sense of jealousy that reared its head. What was that about? Megan wasn't his girlfriend. She was the last woman he should consider having a relationship with.

"Another time, then," Reginald said before he went back into the house.

"Is it really okay with you if Mrs. Crockett's animals stay here?" Megan asked Cade. She nibbled on her bottom lip.

"Yes. But I wasn't kidding about not having time to care for them. This is a working farm and I'm busy twelve or thirteen hours a day. They can stay here, but you'll have to feed them and clean up after them. I'm talking litter boxes for the cats and cleaning up any packages the dogs leave in the lawn. That's nonnegotiable."

"I can do that," she said without hesitation.

Her response surprised him. He couldn't imagine a woman like her with her expensive clothes and perfect hair being willing to clean up after animals. Of course, she might only be saying what she knew he wanted to hear. He'd believe it when he actually saw her in action. "Every day. You won't get weekends off."

She compressed her lips and narrowed her eyes. Still

she looked ridiculously attractive. "I know. I'll be here. I'll come by every day after work."

"And Saturdays and Sundays."

"Yes. Then, too."

"When would you like to bring the animals out?"

"I need to have them examined by Doc J first. Birdie arranged for him to do it this Saturday. That way they can be adopted through Furever Paws. Would it be possible for you to help me bring the animals out here in your truck?"

"Don't want to put the animals in your Mercedes?" He would be the first to admit the car was beautiful, but it would be totally impractical for a farmer to own. Still, he guessed it would work well enough in Spring Forest.

She frowned. "They won't all fit."

"I'll help. Do you need help getting them to the shelter?"

"No. Birdie took care of that."

"Fine. Give me a call when you're ready and I'll meet you at the sanctuary."

This time her brilliant smile was just for him. Despite himself, he smiled in return. They exchanged numbers in case something came up before their scheduled date.

"I'll call you Saturday," Megan said and then got back into her car.

"Saturday," he repeated. No matter how sternly he told himself she was wrong for him, his body stirred in anticipation of seeing her again.

Chapter Four

Megan leaned close to the whimpering dog, murmuring comforting words as Doc J examined him. The dog, an old beagle, turned his eyes to Megan. She easily read the sorrow there. "I know you don't like this, Linus, but it's good for you. Right, Doc?"

Doc J smiled as he gave the dog an injection. "Absolutely."

The dog's whimper turned into a low growl and he bared his teeth at the doctor.

"Didn't like that, huh, boy?" Doc J chuckled, unfazed. Tall and distinguished with a touch of gray at the temples, he was kindhearted and wouldn't be bothered by the dog's aggression. No doubt in his years of practice he'd seen it all.

"I know that hurt, but it's over now and you're all

better," Megan said softly. She rubbed Linus's head and he licked her in return. Laughing, Megan handed the dog off to a volunteer, who attached a leash to the dog's collar and then led him outside.

"Four down, four to go," Doc J said as he washed his hands in the stainless steel sink, something he'd done after each examination. He grabbed a fresh pair of latex gloves from a silver container and slipped them on.

"We finished the cats, so that's technically twelve down."

Doc J laughed. "Trust a lawyer to get all technical on me. I was talking about the dogs."

"I know."

"So how are things going with the Whitaker sisters' case?"

Megan smiled ruefully. "I know you're their good friend, Doc, but I can't discuss the case with you. Client confidentiality."

"No, I don't suppose you can." He lifted Joy-Boy onto the table. The black toy poodle couldn't have weighed more than nine pounds, but by the way he terrorized the other dogs, one would think he was a Great Dane. "But I have to tell you I'm worried about them. They're sweet women and I need you to do your best to protect them."

Rumor around town had it that Doc J was involved with one of the sisters, although there wasn't consensus on which sister held his interest. Megan had seen him with Birdie and Bunny and she hadn't noticed a difference in his behavior with either of them. He treated each woman with the utmost kindness and affection, so if he was in love with one of them, it was a mystery to Megan which one it was.

"Rest assured that I'm doing everything in my power to protect them."

"That's good enough for me."

As they worked, Doc J told her more about Spring Forest. He described his favorite places to eat and the best garage to have maintenance work done on her car. When he'd finished examining and vaccinating the last dog, he snapped off the final pair of latex gloves and tossed them into the trash can, then looked at her. "You're doing a good thing, Megan. Not many people would take on someone else's problem and make themselves responsible for solving it."

"I don't look at finding homes for Mrs. Crockett's pets as a problem. I consider it an opportunity to do a favor for a friend. Kind of like doing free exams on homeless animals." Megan lowered Sunny, a two-year-old yellow Lab, to the floor. She let the dog run around for a minute before fastening the leash to the dog's collar and handing it to the waiting teenage volunteer.

Doc J smiled. "Touché. Take care."

"You too." Megan left the exam room so Doc J could examine his next patient. She needed to let Cade know she was ready, so she went in search of a quiet corner. The shelter was filled with people looking for pets to join their families, so she ended up standing outside in the parking lot. She pulled out her phone and held her hand over the screen. Her stomach tumbled at the thought of seeing Cade again. She didn't understand her continued attraction to the man. Sure, he was good-looking, but as a practice she wasn't interested in people who had a hard time being nice to her. And Cade Battle definitely fit into that category. But since she needed his help transporting the animals to his farm, she called him.

He answered on the first ring, and she wondered briefly if he'd been waiting for her call.

"It's Megan. Doc J finished examining the animals, so we're ready for you to come get us at your convenience."

"I'm actually in the area so I should be there in about fifteen minutes."

"Great."

After Megan ended the call, she gathered the animals and, with the help of four smiling preteen volunteers, took them to where she'd left their crates. They began putting the cats into the pet carriers. The dogs were more interested in sniffing the ground, so Megan let the girls walk them around the lot. It would probably be easier to load them after their crates were on Cade's truck anyway.

It occurred to Megan that she had a problem. She'd ridden over with one of the volunteers.

She didn't have her car with her, which meant she was going to have to ride to the farm with Cade, and she would have to ask him to bring her home later. Either that, or he was going to have to drive her into town now so she could get her car and follow him to the farm. One way or another he was going to be inconvenienced. One more strike against her.

Cade pulled up and she called to the young volunteers to bring the dogs over so they could put them into their cages. He nodded to a couple of people as he made his way over to her. His eyes flickered over her and he raised his eyebrows in apparent surprise. She had to have read that wrong. There was no way he was surprised to see her.

As they loaded the animals into his truck, she explained about her car.

He slammed the tailgate and looked at her. "Ride out to the farm with me now and I'll drop you off at home later."

"Okay." She walked around the truck to climb into the passenger seat. Before she could open her door, he was there, holding it for her. "Wow. Thanks."

He nodded but didn't speak. Apparently his courtesy didn't extend to conversation. Still, it felt good to have someone hold the door for her. As Mrs. Crockett would say, chivalry was a lost art. *I'll tell her about it when I get home.* That thought was followed by a swift, painful dose of reality. Mrs. Crockett was gone. Megan had spent the past week helping her friend sort through a lifetime of memories as she selected which belongings she could pack up and take with her. Mrs. Crockett had shed more than one tear over items that she had to leave behind. She'd pressed her etched glass dessert bowls into Megan's hands, insisting that she take them. She'd said that Megan was the closest thing she had to a daughter, and if she took them, the bowls would still be in the family.

Last night they'd shared one final dinner of Mrs. Crockett's favorites. After dessert they'd sat in Mrs. Crockett's backyard and watched the animals play.

They'd talked well into the night as Mrs. Crockett reminisced about her time in the house that had been her home for many years.

Mrs. Crockett had left this morning. Megan had fought back tears as she'd hugged her friend one last time before Mrs. Crockett's grandniece helped the older woman into her car. Grace had thanked Megan for caring for her great-aunt and promised to keep in touch. Megan had allowed the tears to fall as she watched them drive away, standing on the curb minutes after the car was out of sight. Although Megan knew Mrs. Crockett was going to a place where she would be well cared for, and that Grace was happy to have her great-aunt near, it had still hurt to watch Mrs. Crockett leave. At least Megan had gotten to say goodbye this time.

Megan had expected Cade to try to make at least a bit of small talk as they rode to the farm, but he didn't. Quiet usually didn't bother her—she lived alone and had for years—but there was something about being in Cade's presence and not talking that was unnerving.

She sneaked a peek at him from the corner of her eye. Dressed in a shirt that fit his muscular body so well it might have been tailored for him, and faded jeans that caressed his well-developed thighs, he made her mouth water. If he wore cologne, it was subtle, because she couldn't smell it. Instead, with each breath she inhaled a whiff of clean male. It was quite nice.

She turned to stare out the window. With each passing mile the scenery became more rural. Eventually she began to see fewer houses, and cows and horses began to dot the landscape. When she'd decided to leave New

York, she'd harbored a few worries about moving to such a small town and suffering from culture shock. She'd comforted herself with the knowledge that although Spring Forest was a small town, it was close to Raleigh. If she started to get itchy and in need of a museum or concert, she'd make the short drive to the city. Surprisingly enough, she felt comfortable in Spring Forest and hadn't felt the need to escape yet. It turned out that there was plenty of entertainment in town.

Even more surprising was how at home she'd felt on Cade's farm the other day. Not at home in the sense she hadn't felt since her family's deaths, but at rest. Being on the Battle Lands Farm hadn't felt as strange as it should have. Given the amount of time she was about to spend there, she didn't analyze the feeling, but rather accepted it as an unexpected bonus.

If she was going to spend time on Cade's farm, they were going to bump into each other. She couldn't imagine not at least speaking on those occasions. She might as well break the ice now. "So how's Wilbur?"

He turned and glanced at her for the first time. His brown eyes were filled with confusion. "Who? If you're asking about my dad, his name is Reginald. And he's fine."

"I remember your dad's name and I'm glad to hear that he's well. I was talking about the pig. You were wrestling a pig the first time we met, and I wondered how he was doing. I thought the name Wilbur would suit him, like the pig from the children's book *Charlotte's Web*."

Cade shook his head, but she noticed the corners of

his lips turned up in a smile. That was progress. "The pig's name is Little Piggy. And he was quite delicious."

"You ate Bunny's pig?" Megan screeched, outraged. The Whitaker sisters ran an animal sanctuary. Surely they hadn't intended for their pig to become someone's ham sandwich. They'd wanted the pig to live out its life in joy, rolling around in mud and eating slop or whatever it was pigs did for fun.

Cade laughed. "Of course not. Little Piggy is alive and well on our farm. We're an organic farm and I wouldn't dream of eating food that wasn't."

That was a relief. She'd hate to think he would mislead the sisters. "Do you mind telling me about your farm?"

Cade flashed her a rare grin, and unexpected warmth filled her chest. His smile was lethal, so maybe it was good that he didn't smile at her often. "Of course. Battle Lands Farm has been in our family for four generations. My great-grandfather started out with one hundred or so acres. He left it to my grandfather who added to it when he could. By the time he passed it on to my father, it was nearly two hundred acres. Now we have almost a thousand acres."

"Wow. That's big."

"For North Carolina, maybe. But not as big as farms in other states. And definitely not as big as my brother Chase and I want it to be."

Megan nodded. So he had a brother. This was the first she'd heard of him. That was the bad part about moving someplace new—especially a close-knit community. She didn't know all of the players and how they fit together. Growing up in foster care and being the new kid on more occasions than she'd liked, she'd learned to get the lay of the land before making any moves or asking many questions. The curiosity that her parents and older brother had encouraged and seen as a virtue had become a curse that was often accompanied by painful consequences.

"A few years ago we decided to become a strictly organic farm. Now we produce organic beef and organic free-range chickens and eggs. We also grow organic fruits and vegetables."

"Impressive," Megan said.

Cade glanced at her before returning his gaze to the road. She had the feeling he'd been trying to gauge her sincerity. She couldn't imagine why he'd doubt her. Finally he nodded. "Thanks."

They were nearing Battle Lands Farm and he signaled, then turned into the driveway. As if sensing they were nearing their new temporary home, a couple of the dogs barked. As expected, the others joined in until they were all barking.

"Sorry," Megan said over the noise.

"For what? You didn't set them off."

"True."

"Then don't apologize for something that's not your fault. Okay?"

She nodded.

The house and barns were about a mile from the road. Megan looked out the window, once more impressed by how absolutely beautiful the land was. She'd noticed it the other day, but she'd been too nervous to appreciate the view. Unlike the back of the property, which she imagined was used either for farming or raising animals, the front was simply an enormous lawn. The dark green grass was neatly mown, and enormous leafy trees provided shade. A few rabbits nibbled the grass as squirrels raced around. A glider was situated beneath a large tree and it swung gently in the breeze. Megan imagined many pleasant afternoons and evenings had been spent sitting in that secluded space.

Cade continued driving until they reached the back of the house. He stopped the truck and turned to look at her. "I've cleaned a barn for them. You know better than I which animals get along, so I'll let you choose where each of them will sleep. I imagine you'll put the dogs in one side and the cats in the other."

Megan shook her head. "That's what I would have thought before I met Mrs. Crockett's animals. Not all of the dogs or all of the cats get along with each other so we need to watch for that. And the cats and dogs don't mingle more than they have to. Except for Samson and Delilah. He's a cat and she's a dog. They love each other and sleep together. I don't think they'd appreciate being separated."

Cade shrugged. "This is your show, so do whatever you think is best."

"Okay. Thanks."

Cade let down the tailgate, and they opened the crates to let the animals out. The cats hopped from the truck, then walked around for a bit. When they found a sunny spot on the grass that they liked, they lay down. Once the dogs were on the ground, they stretched their legs and began to sniff around, getting the lay of the land. After a while, they began to chase each other around the yard.

"Oh no," Megan said as they got farther away and showed no sign of coming back.

"What's wrong?"

"The dogs are getting too far away."

"No problem." Cade let out a long whistle. The dogs froze and looked around. Then they came racing back. A couple of the dogs jumped on Cade and he rubbed them. Amazing. He wasn't only a pig wrestler. He was also a dog whisperer. "My dad and I put some cattle panels around the corral fence, so now it's basically a big dog run. They'll be safe there and have plenty of place to run around."

Megan smiled. "You thought of everything."

"I tried. To be honest, I'm not as sure about what to do with the cats."

"I've spent a lot of time with them. They don't do much moving around. As long as there is a sunny spot, they'll be fine. And of course food and a litter box."

"I've already bought that stuff. It's in the barn."

They let the dogs run around for fifteen more minutes before herding them into barn. The dogs knocked into Megan's and Cade's legs in their haste to check out their new surroundings. Cade had purchased stainless steel watering bowls in varying sizes. He showed Megan where the faucet was and then waited while she filled them. Since he'd been adamant that she'd be the one caring for the animals, Megan was surprised when Cade took the filled bowls and placed them against the front wall where all of the animals could easily access them.

A few minutes later the cats meandered into the barn. They strutted around before going to their water bowls and taking a few sips.

Next came the food. When she'd told Cade the brand Mrs. Crockett purchased for her pets, he'd shaken his head. It was an okay brand, he'd told her, but not the best, so she was surprised to see he'd bought the same kind. Maybe after he'd seen how much the food cost, he'd decided it was good enough after all. She tore open the bag and began to scoop it into a bowl.

"Wait."

She paused and turned around. Cade was holding another bag of dog food. She'd seen it at the store and knew that it was very expensive. "Why?"

"I'm switching their food to a different brand. It's not a good idea to just swap it out immediately though. We have to mix the new and the old together. Over the next week we'll gradually decrease the old food until we're feeding them the new brand exclusively."

He showed her how much of each to put in and then stepped back while she filled the bowls. Once that was done, they gave each animal their bowls and stood back while they ate. The dogs gobbled theirs down while the cats nibbled more delicately. Finally dinner was over.

Megan walked down the center aisle beside Cade as he showed her the various empty stalls. They were a lot bigger than she'd expected them to be. "We have way more stalls than you need, so you can put them in whichever way you choose. They're all clean."

"They've lived together for so long I don't think they'll be happy sleeping alone. They might get lonely. It would be best to use five stalls. We can separate the dogs and put them into two stalls and do the same with the cats."

"That's only four."

"Samson and Delilah will get the fifth."

"Okay. Again, you're in charge. I'm just the innkeeper."

They went to the truck and got out the animal beds. When Megan had said goodbye to Mrs. Crockett this morning, Megan had taken all of the blankets the animals slept on with the intention of laundering them. One look had her tossing them into the trash. They'd been so tattered she'd known they wouldn't survive the washing machine's spin cycle. So Megan had gone to the pet supply store and purchased new beds. They'd cost a lot more than she'd expected, but knowing the dogs and cats would be sleeping in comfort made it worth it.

Now she placed the beds in the stalls and was pleased as the dogs and cats walked on their beds before lying down.

"Finished?" Cade asked.

"Not yet." Megan knew how scary it was to be in a strange place. Mrs. Crockett had cried when she'd held her "babies" and said goodbye. The animals must have known that it was a final farewell because several of them had cried, as well. They had to be confused and unsure what would happen next. Although they'd been given food and warm beds, Megan knew it took more than necessities to feel at home. It took love and affection. Patience and caring.

She walked over to Pee-Wee, a tiny elderly dog. Pee-Wee was cautious, preferring to hide behind the other dogs. It had taken Megan a while to win his trust, but once she'd gained it, the dog had allowed her to pick him up and carry him around. She picked him up now and then sat on the floor. "It's going to be okay, Pee-Wee. I know this is a new place and you're scared. That's normal. But I promise you, I'll find a new home for you where you'll be loved and cared for again. It won't be the same, but it will be good."

The dog looked deep into her eyes, and for a moment Megan believed Pee-Wee actually understood her. After a minute he barked once, then slid from her lap and climbed into his bed. He turned around a few times before lying down.

Megan followed the same routine with each animal, assuring them that they would be fine. Although the dogs seemed to need her comfort, the cats had appeared bored by her speech. She knew they were listening, though. Being cats, they just didn't want to let on.

"Done?" Cade asked as she came out of the last stall, which Samson and Delilah were sharing.

"Yes."

"I have to say I've never seen anyone settle animals in like that. Do you intend to do that every night?"

She considered telling him about her experience in foster care and how scary it was go from place to place with seemingly no rhyme or reason. When she saw the mocking expression on his face, she decided against it.

Perhaps he thought it was odd to comfort animals by promising to find them a good home again, and maybe it was. But she didn't think he could understand how disconcerting it was to wake up in one bed in the morning and go to sleep in a different bed that night. After all, he lived on a farm that had been in his family for generations. His roots were as deep and well entrenched as one of those huge trees in his front yard. There were times when she'd felt like a tumbleweed being blown from place to place. Although she didn't know about his mother, she knew his father was alive and well. Living his charmed existence, he wouldn't be able to understand her reality. Not that she begrudged him the good life he enjoyed. She was happy for him. She just wished she could have held on to the one she'd had with her family for a while longer.

She held his gaze. "It's a new place. I just want them to feel comfortable. And I think you would want that, too. You don't want them howling in the middle of the night."

"That's very considerate of you, but unnecessary. I'm usually so exhausted by the time I fall into bed that nothing will wake me."

"Lucky for you." That she did envy. She was a light sleeper and every little sound woke her. She couldn't remember the last time she'd slept through the night.

Cade looked at her for a minute as if debating something. She waited patiently for him to make up his mind. "Would you like to stay for dinner? My father likes you a lot and I know he would enjoy seeing you again."

Surprised, Megan paused. She'd eaten dinner with

Mrs. Crockett just about every night since she'd moved to Spring Forest, and she'd gotten used to have someone to talk to. Megan hadn't been looking forward to eating alone tonight. Eventually she would be alone again, but it was good to be able to put it off for a night. "Thank you. I'd love to."

Chapter Five

Cade led Megan across the backyard to the house, his mind a jumble of confusion. Why had he invited her to share dinner with him and his father? Hadn't he decided that she was wrong for him and that he needed to keep her at a distance? But something about the way she'd talked to the animals, assuring them that they were safe and would find happy homes again, touched him. It had been so unexpected. She'd been so gentle. So loving. It was as if she'd been comforting children. Watching her go from one to the next had worn down his resistance to her, and the invitation had come spilling from his mouth.

As she walked beside him, their hands brushed, and a jolt of electricity shot through his body. He steeled himself, determined to suppress the attraction he felt for her. The type of woman who wore floral perfume when she was going to spend hours on a farm dealing with cats and dogs didn't seem like the type of woman who'd be happy around smelly cattle or a sweaty man who worked with them. He'd ignored that fact once before and suffered the heartbreak. He knew the second time wouldn't be the charm.

Cade held the kitchen door and let her enter. She didn't appear surprised like she had when he'd opened her car door. Apparently the men she'd dealt with in the past lacked common courtesy. Or maybe she hadn't expected a farmer to have manners.

"Megan, what a nice surprise," Cade's dad said when he saw them. He gave the pot of tomato sauce a final stir, then wiped his hands on the towel tied around his waist.

"Thank you. It's good to see you."

"Are the animals all squared away for the night?"

"Yes. Thanks to Cade." Megan glanced at him and to his surprise, his heart swelled with pride at her words. He didn't know why he reacted like she'd said he'd just invented sliced bread.

"You did most of it," he felt compelled to point out.

She smiled brightly at him, and once more his body reacted in a way that displeased him. Unhappy with the way his heart lurched at her words, he didn't return her smile, which eventually faded. He mentally kicked himself. Just because he didn't like being attracted to her didn't give him the right to make her uncomfortable, especially since he'd invited her to dinner. A good host should never be rude.

"Dinner is just about ready," Reginald said. "I take it you're accepting my invitation."

"Yes. If there's enough."

"There's plenty." Reginald turned and looked at Cade. He saw the twinkle in his father's eyes and had no doubt what his father was up to. He was matchmaking. Didn't he realize that was a terrible idea? There was no way his father could have forgotten how gutted Cade had been when his engagement ended. Surely Reginald knew that another city girl was the last thing Cade needed. "Show Megan where she can wash up."

"Follow me," Cade said, turning and going out of the kitchen to the small powder room under the front stairs.

Megan was quiet as they walked through the house. He opened the powder room door and stepped aside, waiting until she'd washed and dried her hands before he did the same. When they returned to the kitchen, dinner was already on the table.

"It smells so good," Megan said. "I love spaghetti."

Cade pulled out her chair and held it for her. She murmured her thanks and he nodded. Reginald had already taken his seat at the head of the table, leaving Cade to sit across from Megan.

"The sauce is an old family recipe," Reginald said. "Not my family, but someone's. I found it in an old church cookbook."

Megan laughed. Her laughter was low and husky, just like her speaking voice.

His father blessed the food and turned to Megan. "We don't stand on ceremony here, so feel free to serve yourself."

They filled their plates with spaghetti, fried catfish, hush puppies and spinach, then dug in.

"So how do you like living in Spring Forest?" Reginald asked.

"I like it. I haven't met very many people, but the ones that I have met have been very friendly. And I like working for Daniel Sutton, which is a plus."

"Where did you move from?"

"New York."

"What do your parents think about you moving so far from home?"

Megan's eyes lost their shine and her shoulders slumped. "My parents and big brother were killed by a drunk driver when I was fourteen. Both of my parents were only children and I had no other family. I was put into foster care."

"I'm sorry," Reginald said.

Cade's mind reeled with shock. She'd lost her family and been ripped from her home and all that had been familiar to her. No wonder she was so caring with the displaced animals. She probably related to their plight because their experience was similar to hers. His stomach churned as he recalled making fun of the way she'd babied the animals. No doubt someone had said the same words to her. Or had she only wished someone had comforted her like that?

"They were great parents and my brother was the best brother anyone could have. I try to live my life in a way that would make them all proud." She lifted her glass to her lips and took a long swallow. He sensed that she wanted to change the subject. From the way her hand shook, he knew discussing her parents' and brother's deaths was painful for her.

"I haven't known you long, but from what I've seen, I'm sure they're very proud of you," Cade said. Just look at the way she stepped in to help her elderly neighbor, taking on the responsibility for sixteen animals. It took a special person to do that. It didn't mean she wasn't still a city girl with city girl sensibilities. And it definitely didn't mean she was someone he should want to become involved with. It simply meant she was a considerate person.

"Thank you for saying that," Megan said quietly. She swirled the ice in her glass of lemonade for a few long seconds. Then she looked up at him. "Can you tell me more about the farm?"

"Sure. What do you want to know?"

She shrugged. "I don't know enough about farms to ask an intelligent question. Just tell me what you think would interest me. Or better yet, tell me what you like best about being a farmer."

"How much time do you have?" Cade asked with a laugh.

"You're the one driving me home, so…" she shrugged and her voice trailed off.

He pushed his empty plate to the center of the table and leaned his forearm on the table. "I'll give you general information about the Battle Lands Farm. I already told you how many acres we have. We employ twenty full-time employees who help care for the livestock and crops. Since our animals are organic, we allow them to graze on the open land. They need lots of space and water. We absolutely do not use any antibiotics or steroids of any kind. We do things the natural way. The humane way."

She nodded.

Animal cruelty was one of the things that set Cade off. He took a deep breath and then blew it out. "Sorry. I didn't mean to go on a rant."

"Don't apologize for caring about how animals are treated. It shows you have a good heart, which is something that's often lacking in the world these days."

"In addition to a good heart, my son has a good head on his shoulders, which is why I want to transfer ownership of the farm to him and his brother," Reginald said.

"If you want, I can handle the legal work for you," Megan offered.

"Really? Then we would like to hire you," Reginald said before Cade could get a word in edgewise.

"Consider me hired." Megan smiled and held out her hand for Reginald to shake. She then held it out to Cade, and he had no choice but to take it. Her hand was just as soft and warm as he remembered, and he wished he had a reason to hold it longer—which just made him drop it all the faster. "I'll call you tomorrow to schedule a meeting with the three of you. That is, if your other son wants to be present as well."

"Sounds good. Chase lives in Raleigh, but I'll call and see when he's available." Reginald rose. "I'll leave you young people to talk. It was nice seeing you again, Megan."

"I really like your dad," Megan said when she and Cade were alone. There was a longing in her voice, but now that he knew about her past, he understood it. No doubt she was missing her own father.

"He's a good man and a good father."

Megan didn't respond. Instead she stared out the window. The sun had long since set and the moon and stars had taken over the sky. He wished he knew what she was thinking, but he didn't have a clue. While she admired the night, he took the opportunity to admire her. Dressed in denim shorts that showcased her long, slender legs and a cotton blouse. She still managed to look elegant and sophisticated.

Finally she looked at him. "I know you need to get up early tomorrow, so I suppose we should get going."

It was getting late, but he wasn't ready for her to leave. He was actually enjoying her company. But it wouldn't make good sense for either of them to stay up too late tonight only to be exhausted tomorrow. Not to mention that he needed to resist the attraction simmering beneath the surface. He'd been there and done that and was in no hurry to repeat that experience. But as they walked to the truck together, he couldn't silence the hum of desire surging through his body.

He heard her muttering but couldn't make out her words. He leaned in closer but still was unable to understand what she was saying. "What did you say?"

She blinked. "Sorry, I was talking to myself. I wanted to make a wish on a star, but there are so many of them I can't figure out which one I saw first. So I was just telling myself that I should have paid closer attention."

"The sky is filled with stars. Just pick one and wish."

"If only it was that easy. The poem says *first* star

I see, not any random star I happen to spot. I guess I could make a wish on any of them, but it wouldn't come true. Only the first star is magical."

He was familiar with the kids' rhyme and had wished upon stars when he was a boy. He didn't know any kid who hadn't. But he didn't remember taking the poem as literally as she was doing. And unlike her, he hadn't expected the wishes to come true. It had all been done in good fun. "Well, choose one anyway and maybe you'll get lucky."

She shook her head. "It doesn't work that way. But that's okay. There's always tomorrow."

"What were you going to wish?" This was a ridiculous conversation, yet he was continuing it. Maybe knowing what she'd wanted to wish would help him understand her better. And for some unknown reason, he wanted to know her better.

"I can't tell you or it won't come true."

"I thought that only applied to birthday candles."

"It's the universal law of wishes. Any wish that you reveal won't come true."

"So does that mean you can tell people what you wished after they come true, or does that put a hex on all future wishes? Do the fairies or elves or whoever the wish-granters are know you won't keep them a secret so they refuse to grant any in the future?"

"It's okay to tell after it has been granted," she said seriously. "That testimony gives encouragement to others waiting for their own wishes to come true."

He shrugged. This was too deep for him. Maybe there was a book of rules. He still couldn't believe he'd

just had a conversation about wishes. Even more unbelievable was how much he'd enjoyed it. When they
reached his truck, he helped her inside before getting
behind the wheel and driving her home. Megan wasn't
turning out to be what he'd expected her to be. She was
a bit of a mystery. He didn't like leaving puzzles un-
solved, so he knew he'd have to figure her out. She'd be
coming to the farm every day, so he'd have time. The
prospect of seeing her that often wasn't an unpleasant
one. In fact, he was actually looking forward to it.

Megan dropped her briefcase onto a chair in her
living room, then dashed into her bedroom, kicking
off her heels and unbuttoning her blouse as she went.
A client had called with concerns just as she'd been
leaving for the day. The conversation had last nearly
forty-five minutes. Ordinarily Megan was glad to talk
to clients—that was part of her job, after all—but today's call couldn't have come at a worse time. This
was the first day she was going to Battle Lands Farm
to take care of the animals. She'd phoned Cade's cell
twice to let him know she was running late, but he
hadn't answered. He probably thought she wasn't going
to show up, leaving him alone with the responsibility for sixteen cats and dogs he hadn't wanted in the
first place.

She and Cade had gotten along well last night. She
didn't know why he'd had a negative opinion of her, but
she'd arrived home believing she'd changed his percep-
tion of her. She'd hoped to build on last night's progress
by proving to him that she was reliable. Showing up late

would no doubt have him thinking poorly of her again. She needed to get to the farm fast.

Thank goodness she'd had the foresight to lay out her clothes before she left for work this morning, so it only took a minute for her to change from her suit into her jeans and T-shirt. At the last minute she grabbed a jacket just in case it got cool this evening, then ran to her car. As she drove down the street, she glanced at the house where Mrs. Crockett used to live and her heart pinched.

Grace had kept her word and phoned Megan as soon as she and Mrs. Crockett arrived at the senior living facility. Megan had even spoken briefly to her former neighbor, who'd said she believed she'd be happy in her new home. And that she was glad to have Grace's family nearby. Megan had been relieved, but she still missed the older woman who'd become a good friend in a short period of time. One more person Megan had loved and lost. But part of Mrs. Crockett was still here, in the animals she loved so dearly. And those animals were waiting for Megan right now.

She drove as fast as she dared down the highway, her tension mounting with each passing minute. She didn't take an easy breath until she saw the large sign announcing that she'd arrived at the Battle Lands Farm. She slowed and then pulled into the long driveway. Despite knowing that Cade was probably irritated with her, her heart felt lighter as she neared the house and barns.

"I'm so sorry," she said as she jumped from the car. "I know I'm late."

Cade ignored her apology. "The animals are waiting."

"What kind of day did they have? Are they settling in all right?"

"I don't know. I'm not an animal psychiatrist. Besides I had other things to do today than watch them. This is a working farm, remember."

"Oh." She tried not to sound as disappointed as she felt. It wasn't as if being concerned about these animals was his job. He was only providing the lodging and food, not the attention they needed. It would be up to her to give the pets love and affection.

The cats were lying around in the remaining light, apparently content. She wondered if they'd spent the day sunning themselves. Megan took a few minutes to give them individual attention. Samson wasn't around, but that wasn't cause for concern. No doubt he was hanging out with Delilah in the corral. The dogs tolerated his presence much better than the cats tolerated Delilah's.

When she stood and turned, Cade was still standing there. He'd obviously been watching her. Had he expected her to immediately start cleaning up after the animals? She'd get to that in time. To her it was more important to take care of the animals' emotional needs before seeing to their physical ones.

He shoved his hands into the pocket of his jeans. "If you want to know how the animals are adjusting to living here, you can check with my dad. He was around the house all day and spent some time with them."

Megan smiled tentatively. Maybe Cade wasn't as unfeeling as he appeared. Of course, it was hard to be certain about anything when it came to him. His behavior was so inconsistent. It was as if he was engaged in some internal battle. She'd always thought the images of a devil on one shoulder and an angel on the other, each trying to influence someone's behavior, were ridiculous. Cade had her reconsidering that opinion. If ever a man was conflicted, it was him.

Not that he was alone in being torn. She was suffering from the same affliction. Despite her hard and fast rule about never trying to win the heart of someone who wasn't inclined to love her, she couldn't stop wondering "what if" when it came to Cade Battle.

When he'd dropped her off last night, she'd imagined what it would be like to kiss him good-night. Her heart had nearly leaped from her chest at the ridiculous notion. Not that she could ever find out now, even if he ever did show interest. He was a client and she had a strict rule against dating clients or former clients. It was imperative that she keep her professional and personal lives separate. She'd worked hard to get her education and become a lawyer. Her career meant everything to her and she had no intention of jeopardizing it. Not that Cade had given even the slightest indication that he was interested in her as a woman. Still, it was good to remind herself of her rule before she let her imagination lead her down a path she shouldn't travel.

"Thanks. I'll talk to your dad before I leave. Now I think I'll play with the dogs for a bit before I clean up after them. Then I'll feed them. If that's okay with you."

"It's fine."

She walked toward the corral where the dogs had spent the day. She'd only taken a couple of steps when she noticed that Cade was walking beside her. Taking his presence as a sign that he was making an effort to be friendly, she decided to do the same. "How was your day?"

He seemed surprised by her question, and a few seconds passed before he answered. "Fine. July is one of our busier months. The days are longer but sometimes it feels like there won't be enough daylight to get everything done."

"Well, you don't have to worry about the cats and dogs. I intend to keep my word to take care of them so there won't be even more on your plate."

"I know that. And if I seemed hard or unfeeling the other day, I apologize."

"An apology isn't necessary, but I appreciate it just the same."

"And I'm also sorry for snapping at you just now. It was totally uncalled for."

She nodded. "Accepted."

They reached the corral and he opened the gate for her. Although a couple of the dogs lifted their heads when she entered, most of them remained lying down. Were they sick? She looked at Cade, who grinned sheepishly. "I might have thrown a few balls around with them while I was waiting for you to show up. They seemed to enjoy it." And just like that, a part of her heart that she'd intended to protect at all costs began to sing. She struggled to cut off the music. She wasn't going to make another mistake.

"Mrs. Crockett's backyard was pretty small, so there wasn't much room for them to run around. Having all this space must seem like heaven to them." She'd tucked a couple of balls and a rope in a bag, intending to play with the dogs for a while herself. That plan went by the wayside quickly. The dogs were exhausted. They'd probably spent a good deal of the day chasing each other.

She called the dogs and they walked over, wagging their tails when she rubbed them. A couple barked and ran around her feet before sitting down. As she'd done with the cats, she gave each one individual attention, using their names as she talked to them.

Several stainless steel bowls were filled with water. Imagining that the bowls had been sitting out for a while, Megan grabbed one to add fresh water. To her surprise the water was cold. "I gave the dogs water a few minutes before you arrived," Cade explained. "I didn't know how much later you were going to be."

"Thanks."

There were several chew toys lying around the corral, and she looked at Cade, who shrugged. "My dad. He thought the dogs would like toys to play with when they got tired from running around. And when you go into the barn, you'll notice some cat toys as well as a couple of cat mansions."

"Cat mansions?"

"Yep. Two of them."

"More gifts from your dad?"

"He wouldn't buy for the dogs and leave the cats with nothing. That would be playing favorites, something he would never do."

Megan leaned against the rail fence encircling the large grassy corral and looked out over the vast farm.

"Your dad is really great. You're so lucky to have him around."

"I know. He's one of a kind. When Chase and I were growing up, all of our friends wanted to hang out here because of how cool my parents were."

"What happened to your mother, if you don't mind me asking?"

"She died last year. Cancer."

"I'm sorry."

He blew out a breath, and she knew he was gathering his emotions. When he spoke again, his voice was choked. "It came out of nowhere. Mom had always been healthy. She didn't drink or smoke and she watched what she ate. Living on a farm, she got plenty of fresh air and exercise. She did everything right and still got sick. She fought hard to beat it. She did chemo and had radiation treatments, but nothing worked. All they did was make her sicker. Day by day she got weaker and weaker and there was nothing we could do to help her. It seemed as though she was sick for a long time, but the end came so fast. It just happened all of a sudden. One minute she was there and the next she was gone."

Megan could tell from his bewildered tone that he was still trying to make sense of something that didn't make sense and never would. She'd fought that same fight for years before she'd finally accepted the truth. In life some things happened without rhyme or reason. Trying to comprehend the incomprehensible would only lead to heartache. Yet she also knew that acceptance was a process, so she didn't try to impart any words of wisdom. And who knew, maybe he was the rare person who would find a way to make sense of it all.

"I'm sorry," she repeated, at a loss for anything else to say.

"The neighbors were great, which is one of the reasons Dad was so insistent that we pay it forward by taking in Mrs. Crockett's animals."

"Right. Speaking of them… I'd better get to cleaning up before the light fades."

She'd brought a pooper scooper and Cade provided a bucket, so she got busy cleaning the corral. Pee-Wee barked softly when she came near him, but other than that, the dogs largely ignored her. When she was done, she lugged the bucket to the gate. She had absolutely no idea what she was supposed to do with the poop.

She was opening the gate when Cade returned. He took the bucket from her.

"Thanks. I'm not sure what I'm supposed to do with it."

"I'll take care of it."

"Are you sure? I promised not to add to your workload."

He laughed. "It won't take more than a minute to dispose of this. I can spare that much time."

"Thanks. I'll get started on the litter boxes."

"Be my guest."

Once she'd scooped the litter boxes, she washed her hands. Cade had written measurements for the food, so she mixed the old and new food into the bowls and set them out. The cats, except for Samson, who was hanging out with the dogs, had followed her into the barn and immediately went to their bowls to eat. Megan was about to go and get the dogs when she heard them running into the barn beside Cade.

"I thought I would help you out a little."

"Thanks." The dogs raced to their bowls and began to gobble down their food. Instead of going back to whatever he'd been doing, Cade leaned against the door, his arms folded over his muscular chest. No doubt he was used to the commotion a bunch of animals caused when they ate. She'd never been at Mrs. Crockett's house at mealtime, so yesterday was the first time she'd witnessed the animals eat.

"The dogs sure do eat fast," Megan said.

"You should have seen them this morning."

Megan slapped a hand on her forehead. "I didn't come out this morning. It didn't even cross my mind that I needed to."

"How do you think the dogs and Samson got to the corral? Someone had to let them out and give them water all day."

"I'm sorry. I didn't mean to add to your workload. I'll stop by in the mornings from now on."

"That's not necessary. My dad helped. To be honest, I think he likes having them here. When I got back from taking you home last night, I found him in the barn, checking on them. It's good for him to have things around for him to love and care for."

"He has you."

"Yes, but I can take care of myself. Besides, I don't live this close to him."

"You don't live here? I thought you did."

"I live on the farm, but I have my own house. It's about twenty minutes away on the eastern section of our property. It can get pretty quiet and empty around here once everyone has gone home. I know that's the time when my dad misses my mother the most, so I eat dinner with him a few times a week to keep him from getting lonely."

Megan's heart swelled at Cade's words. "You are such a good son."

He seemed embarrassed by her praise and looked down at his shoes for a moment. When his gaze returned to hers, it was filled with an emotion she couldn't name. "I didn't always appreciate him. Or my mother, for that matter. It took losing her to realize how much she meant to me. Of course, it was too late to show her. I'm determined not to make the same mistake with my father."

She nodded. Not a day passed that she didn't wish she'd had more time with her family and the ability to tell them how much she loved them, so she understood what he meant. "I'm sure he appreciates having you around."

"I hope so."

The animals finished eating and began to wander around the barn. The sun had faded and the once hot day turned cooler. Most of the cats migrated to the cat mansions, as Cade had referred to them, and found places to lie down. There were two identical cat houses, each with four enclosed cubbies, four round beds, and several thick scratching posts. He'd placed one in each of their large stables between the beds she'd bought. The cats were definitely living in the lap of luxury.

The dogs, on the other hand, weren't as ready to settle down, so she and Cade let them go outside, where they walked around the corral for a bit. While the dogs enjoyed the outdoors, Megan and Cade leaned against the rail. Neither of them spoke, but the silence between them was companionable. After a while the dogs began to wind down and one by one came to the gate. Once the dogs were in the barn, they settled into their beds. Megan once more said good night to each of the pets before going to her car. She was surprised to see Cade waiting for her.

"I guess it's a wrap," she said, stretching. She covered a yawn.

"One day down, countless more to go."

"I need to check Rebekah and find out how the adoption process works. Hopefully she'll have an adoption fair soon and families will fall in love with the pets. Or maybe when space opens up they'll be able to move to the shelter. Whatever happens, I'll let you know so I don't disrupt your life more than is necessary."

He smiled as he opened her car door. "Don't worry about it. A little disruption is good for the soul."

That comment caught her off guard. He might think disruption was all right, but she'd had enough to last a lifetime. Now she just wanted a calm and predictable life.

Chapter Six

Cade was always an early riser, but he woke earlier than usual and headed to his father's house. After parking his truck in his usual spot beneath a tall tree, he checked on the animals. As they had yesterday, the cats ignored him. He got the feeling they believed the barn was their domain and he was the intruder. If there was one thing this hotel for animals gig was teaching him, it was that cats were not to be bothered unless they wanted to be bothered. The dogs, on the other hand…well, he was learning why they were considered man's best friend. The minute he walked into the barn, they began barking and jumping around his feet, obviously thrilled to see him.

He let the dogs into the corral so they could run a bit and then got their food and water ready. Hooking his foot on the bottom rail, he watched them play for a few minutes before he went into his father's kitchen. Reginald was pouring a mug of coffee.

"Good morning, son." Reginald filled a second mug with coffee and passed it over.

"Thanks." Cade breathed in the aroma before taking a sip. Perfect. Nobody made coffee as good as his father's. When he'd moved into his own house four years ago, Cade had followed his father's directions to the letter but couldn't duplicate the brew. After many unsuccessful attempts, he'd finally given up and started joining his parents in the mornings.

"Do you have time for breakfast?"

"Of course." Cade sat at the table and stretched his legs in front of him. Though he couldn't make coffee, Cade was an excellent cook. His mother had spent hours teaching him and he'd memorized most of her recipes. Still, Reginald was the king in his kitchen now and a firm believer that too many cooks could spoil the meal. To Reginald, two was one too many. So instead of helping, or getting in the way, as Reginald called it, Cade watched as his father chopped mushrooms, tomatoes and onions for omelets, then shredded a brick of cheese. When his father started to fry a ham steak, Cade recalled Megan's appalled reaction when he'd told her Little Piggy had been delicious and he laughed out loud.

"Something tickle your funny bone?" Reginald asked.

"Yes. I was just remembering something Megan said."

"Well, don't keep it a secret."

Cade recounted the story and he and his father

laughed together. When he'd stopped laughing, Reginald stirred a splash of milk into the eggs and then poured the mixture into a frying pan. He kept his back to Cade while he worked. "Megan is a nice girl."

Cade grunted his reply, signaling his disinterest in continuing the conversation.

"Pretty, too. Being new to town, she can't know many people." He added the vegetables and cheese to the pan. "And from the sound of it, she spent most of her time with Mrs. Crockett and her menagerie. Now, Mrs. Crockett was a nice woman, but I don't imagine a ninety-year-old woman showed her much of Spring Forest."

Cade knew his father well, so this conversation, while unwanted, was not unexpected. What Cade didn't know was the best way to end it. He decided to give silence a try.

Reginald slid the omelet onto a plate and immediately got to work on the next. He dropped four slices of bread into the toaster and continued his matchmaking without missing a beat. "Now, a young man like you could show her a few of the sights."

"I'm busy, Dad. I'm already taking care of her animals in the morning even though I don't have time for the hassle." Not that it was entirely a hassle. He was discovering that he liked the animals even the cats who probably couldn't care less how he felt about them. He hadn't had a pet growing up, not unless you counted his horse, so it was kind of nice to have animals around that showed affection. He had a soft spot for Delilah. And Delilah seemed to like him, too. Whenever he was near, she'd follow him around or sit at his feet.

"That's true. The farm is busy this time of year." Reginald said, taking the second omelet from the pan and sliding it onto a plate. He added toast and ham to each plate and carried them to the table, setting one in front of Cade and keeping the other for himself. "Still, Megan is alone now and needs someone to show her around."

Cade nodded and dug into his food. "This is good. Thanks."

"Maybe that Jamison kid can take her around," Reginald mused.

"You mean Keith?"

"Yep. He's a nice young man."

"He got married four months ago. I doubt his wife would appreciate you setting him up on a date." Reginald knew very well that Keith had gotten married. He'd gone to the ceremony. He was just trying to goad Cade into hanging around with Megan. Cade wasn't going to fall for it.

"I suppose not. Well, I'll think of someone. It's not right for a young girl to be all alone in a strange town. Actually, when you think of it, she's all alone in the world."

Cade sighed. Apparently he wasn't as immune to his father's plotting as he'd believed. Something in his chest had torn when Megan told them about losing her entire family. He couldn't imagine how she'd endured the pain. He'd wanted to crawl into a hole and stay there when his mother died. Even then he'd still had his father and Chase. She'd lost both parents and her brother in one fell swoop.

Cade knew his father was playing dirty, but what he was saying was true. Megan had no one. Cade didn't for a moment imagine that she was friendless—she was too caring for that—but it was possible she hadn't made close friends yet in Spring Forest. That would make for a lonely life. "I'll show her around."

"That's good of you, Cade."

He aimed his fork at his father to make his point. "But it won't be right away. I really am swamped around here. And every free minute that I have, I spend trying to make the farm-to-table plans a reality."

"You'll do it. I have complete faith in your abilities."

"Thanks, Dad." As Cade basked in his father's praise, he realized how fortunate he was. He still had his father's love and support. "And I'll find time for Megan."

"Good."

Not that it would be a hardship. Who would find it difficult to be around a beautiful woman with a kind heart? That would be easy. The hard part would be keeping himself from doing something foolish like falling for her.

Megan closed her office door and quickly changed into a pair of faded jeans and a pink-and-green-striped top. She'd brought the clothes with her just in case she got held up at the office again. It was important to her that Cade knew she respected his time. Although she didn't have a clear picture of what his day entailed, she knew it was important and time-consuming. Running a farm sounded interesting and she wanted to know about his job. Hopefully he would tell her more.

She was still trying to get to know him, which wasn't easy. He hadn't been very friendly when they first met, but she had been pleasantly surprised by his attitude yesterday. He'd been very kind to her, and to the animals. She hoped that the Cade she'd spent time with yesterday was the real one.

She grabbed the hanger holding her suit in one hand and opened the door with the other. Stepping into the hall, she waved goodbye to Daniel, who was on his office phone, then left. Once in the car, she rolled down her windows and let the sweet breeze blow in.

When Megan arrived on the farm, she drove to the back of the house and parked near the barn. She looked around, but Cade was nowhere to be found. Her heart sank, but she reminded herself that he had to work. Hadn't he told her that he was too busy to take care of sixteen cats and dogs? Pushing aside her disappointment, she looked for the cats. She'd expected them to be lazing in the sun, but they weren't. Perhaps they were in the barn playing with their toys or in the cat mansions. She looked in the stalls, but they were empty. She searched the entire barn, but they were nowhere to be found.

"Now, where did you get off to?"

Megan picked up her pace as she headed for the corral. The dogs and Samson were there and they greeted her enthusiastically. She rubbed each of the dogs while Samson wound around her legs. Although she hadn't really expected the other cats to be here, she'd hoped. "Where are the other kitties?"

She turned in a slow circle, hoping for a glimpse of

the missing felines. Nothing. She was going to have to search for them. Although she'd been concerned about the dogs getting lost on the farm, it had never occurred to her that the cats would be the ones to wander away. What if they got lost and she couldn't find them? Or what if they ended up with the cattle and got squashed or stampeded?

Megan's knowledge of the layout of the farm was limited to the house and barns. There were acres and acres of land she hadn't even seen, much less explored. Since she had no idea where the cats would go, she chose a random direction and walked that way. It was slow going because she stopped and listened for purring every few feet. After fifteen minutes of fruitless searching, she was about to turn around when she heard meowing. She followed the sound and found the cats lying in tall grass. She called their names, but of course, being cats, they didn't deem her worthy of a response. Princess did look up before licking her front paws.

There was no way she was going to be able to carry them all, so they were going to have to walk on their own. "Okay, little kitties, it's time to go back."

Bella was nearest to her, so Megan nudged her. The cat gave Megan a dirty look before standing. Megan then proceeded to poke all of the other cats until they were standing, although some of them were only stretching. Megan had a feeling it wasn't going to get any better than this. "Let's get back to the barn."

Megan took two steps but none of the cats followed her. Dogs were so much easier. She considered running back to the barn and getting some treats, but decided against it. What if the cats decided to wander some-where else while she was gone? She might not find them again. Going back, she began to push the cats in the way she wanted them to go. Some followed but others sat back down, and Felix went in an entirely different direction. Megan chased after him. "Oh, no you don't."

After about ten minutes of chasing cats and urging them into the right direction, Megan had barely moved more than a hundred feet. At this rate she'd never get back to the barn. She began to sing a fast song. Perhaps playing the role of the Pied Piper would encourage the cats to follow quickly. It didn't.

"This is so ridiculous," she said to no one in partic-ular. The cats certainly weren't paying her any mind.

"I agree."

Cade's voice startled her and she jumped and turned to look at him. There was a wide grin on his face. She was transfixed by his smile for a few seconds, which was long enough for two of the cats to sneak off in op-posite directions. "Come back here, you rascals."

She chased after Felix while Cade sprinted after Bella. They caught their cats and brought them back to the other five, who had begun to wander off. Fortu-nately they hadn't gotten too far. Rather than put down their escapees, they carried them to the yard, using their legs to prod the others in the right direction.

Once they were back in the yard, Megan heaved a heavy sigh. "That was nuts. It was like…"

"Herding cats?" Cade offered.

Megan laughed. "Yes. I never really gave much thought to that term before. I've used it, of course, but

I've never thought what it would actually be like to try and herd cats. Now that I know? If I never have to try that again it will be too soon."

Cade laughed with her. The sound sent tingles shimmying down her spine. What was it about this man that made her feel so giddy and light? So happy and peaceful? She'd never experienced anything like this with Tim and they'd been engaged. Now she wondered how big a role his loving family had played in her attraction to him. His mother and sisters had been wonderful and she'd loved being included in their group. But Tim's touch had never made her knees go weak. Kissing him had been pleasant but not earth-shattering. Just casually brushing against Cade made her knees turn to goo and left her questioning her ability to stand.

"I wonder what made them decide to venture so far away from the house," Cade said. Clearly he didn't understand felines any better than she did.

"I don't know. But whatever it is, I hope they don't do it again tomorrow. They made dinner late."

Megan filled the water and food bowls, then hurriedly completed her cleanup duties. While she worked, she lectured the cats about wandering off. The speech was more for herself than the cats because she knew they weren't listening. Still, she felt better having warned them of the dangers in the world.

When she was finished with the cats, she went outside, closing the barn door behind her. She found Cade in the corral, throwing balls to the dogs. He rubbed them briskly whenever they brought the balls back. He took off running a few times and laughed when the dogs caught him. He seemed so carefree, unlike the grumpy man she'd first met.

Samson climbed the fence and walked along the top rail until he reached Megan. She picked him up, then rubbed him. Although she liked all of the animals and tried to treat them all equally, she loved Samson a little bit more.

Cade tossed the balls a few more times, then let the dogs keep them. He wandered over to the fence, Delilah by his side. When he reached Megan, Cade climbed over the fence, then stood beside her. "Your favorite?"

"There's just something about Samson. He's such a cool cat."

"Don't tell the other dogs, but Delilah is my favorite."

Smiling, Megan pretended to lock her lips. "Your secret is safe with me."

"Do you have plans for the night?"

"Not at all. If I'm lucky I'll find something on TV worth watching. If not, there's always sleep."

"Would you like to have dinner with me?"

Surprised she took a deep breath before answering. "Yes."

"Then let's put the dogs and Samson in the barn and get going."

Once the animals were settled for the night, Megan walked toward the house. Cade put a hand on her arm, stopping her. "My truck is over here."

"Oh. I thought you meant your father's house."

"No. I meant my house. Do you want to change your answer?"

She shook her head. "Not at all. I still want to have dinner with you."

After they'd gotten into the pickup, Cade drove down a back road Megan hadn't known existed. It was mostly dirt with grass in the middle, so maybe it wasn't so much a road as a path. As they bumped along, Megan looked out the window at the beautiful farm. She was impressed by what she saw. There were acres and acres of tomatoes, peppers, bush beans, onions, and other plants that she couldn't identify. Until this moment she hadn't had a complete grasp on just how big a farm this was, nor had she appreciated just how much work it had to take to keep it going. Cade carried a lot of responsibility on his shoulders. The farm provided the livelihood for him and Reginald as well as their employees' families.

Megan looked at him with new appreciation. "This is absolutely amazing."

He seemed almost embarrassed. "Thanks."

They drove a few more minutes before Cade slowed and parked in front of a pale yellow house. Unlike the main house, this one was small. Quaint. She loved it on sight.

Cade opened the front door and she stepped into a small entry that opened onto a decent-sized living room. She'd expected him to have leather furniture or no furniture at all, so she was pleasantly pleased by his fabric sectional and coordinating chair. A breeze blew through the open windows. There were no window treatments, but if she had the view he had, she wouldn't cover it up with curtains or blinds either.

She followed Cade through a dining room and past a

flight of stairs, which led to the second floor. He pointed out the powder room before they reached the kitchen. It was modern with soapstone counters, glistening appliances, and a large farmhouse sink. On the floor near the back door were two stainless steel bowls filled with water. She looked at Cade and he shrugged. "I told you I really like Delilah. I brought her home with me yesterday. Of course she wouldn't come without Samson, so he came, too."

Megan smiled. Cade was more of a softy than he'd let on. "Where did they sleep?"

He grinned sheepishly. "I brought their beds home with me last night and took them back to the barn this morning."

"Why?"

He laughed. "I didn't want my dad to think I was playing favorites by bringing home two animals and leaving the rest."

Megan wondered if he would do the same thing tonight but decided not to ask. She didn't want to be disappointed if he said no. She'd rather live with the fantasy where Cade let Samson and Delilah move in with him permanently and they all lived happily ever after. Of course there should be a woman in that picture as well to complete the family, and for a brief moment she imagined being that woman. She forced the thought away. It would only lead to disappointment. For all she knew, Cade had a girlfriend.

She turned her focus back to Cade, who was pulling pans from cabinets. "Do you need help with dinner?"

"No. I actually enjoy cooking. My mother insisted

that Chase and I learn how to cook. I'm pretty good if I do say so myself."

Megan's mother had begun to teach her how to cook, too. Unfortunately the lessons had ended when her mother died. None of her foster mothers had been interested in spending time in the kitchen with a silent kid. It wasn't until she met Tim and began spending time with his mother that she once more had someone devoted to helping her improve her skills. Now she was a pretty decent cook, and though her repertoire was small, the meals she put together were quite tasty.

"What are we having?"

"Chicken marsala, mashed potatoes and a salad made with vegetables I picked from my backyard garden today."

"Impressive. Do you really have your own garden or are you talking about the farm vegetables?"

"I have a garden for my own personal use. And we have a several greenhouses as well."

"This farm is amazing."

He pounded the chicken until it was flat and then dredged it in flour. A moment later he had it cooking in the pan. "There's more that I want to do."

"Like what?"

"Have you heard of the farm-to-table movement?"

"Yes, but I only know the basics. It's where farmers sell directly to restaurants, right?"

"Yes. The produce is freshly picked and is used immediately. The food is fresher so it has more nutrients and tastes better. There's no middle man so the restaurant's cost is lower, which allows them to charge less for their meals. The lower price in turn allows more people, especially those with lower budgets for dining out, to enjoy a delicious meal they might not otherwise have been able to afford. It's a win for everyone involved."

"That's a wonderful idea. When are you going to start it?"

"I'm working on it. I've solidified the plans and I've worked out the harvesting schedule. With the greenhouses I can provide produce all year round. Now I've just got to get some contracts and of course market to potential customers."

"I would be happy to draw up the contracts for you. I am a lawyer, after all."

"Are you any good?"

He winked at her when he asked his question, but even though Megan knew he was kidding, she answered him seriously. "Yes. I received my undergraduate degree in finance and my law degree from Howard University. I graduated summa cum laude both times. I was hired by a major law firm in New York, where I worked for almost three years before I moved to North Carolina last month."

"Impressive. I guess that's your way of saying you can handle my piddling contracts."

"No. That's my way of saying that if you trust me to draft your very important business contracts, you'll be hiring someone who is qualified."

"Okay. In the words of my father, consider yourself hired."

They talked about sports and favorite television shows while he cooked. Though he didn't need her assistance cooking, he was more than happy for her to set the table. When he told her he had a flower garden, she cut several blooms. He didn't own a vase, so she arranged them in a glass pitcher. She was setting them on the table just as Cade announced that the food was done. He served her first and then himself.

She felt his eyes on her as she took her first bite. Her taste buds reacted immediately. "This is absolutely delicious. You have to give me the recipe."

"I'll do that."

They continued their conversation, moving on to favorite books. Megan was surprised to discover that she and Cade both favored mysteries, although he also liked true crime stories, a genre she would never touch. By the time they finished their dessert of mixed fresh berries and sweet cream, Megan felt they were on their way to becoming friends.

As it was getting late, he drove her back to her car. She'd told herself not to ask but she couldn't help herself. "Are you taking Samson and Delilah home with you?"

He grinned. "Yep."

"Good." She was glad that Samson and Delilah were going to be sleeping in a house tonight. It was as if they were creating her fantasy family. Oh how she wished she could make her own fantasy about becoming part of a family come true, too.

Chapter Seven

The next few days were enjoyable and they sped by. After completing her legal work at the office, Megan would change clothes and head to the farm for what was rapidly becoming her favorite part of the day. After she'd finish her chores, she and Cade would toss the ball to the dogs, letting them run around and burn off excess energy. If the cats were inclined, Megan and Cade would give them attention, as well. Once all of the animals were settled for the night, she and Cade would either eat dinner with Reginald or the two of them would go to Cade's house and cook dinner together.

Today was Saturday and Megan didn't have to go into the office. Even so, she got up early, ate a quick breakfast, and drove to the farm. It was her intention to arrive early enough to feed the animals so Cade wouldn't have to. He'd said he didn't mind doing it, but she didn't want to take advantage of his kindness any more than she already had. Yesterday Rebekah told her that the shelter had room for two cats and one dog, so Megan could bring three of Mrs. Crockett's animals to the shelter. Now Megan was faced with deciding which ones would get the opportunity to find a new family right away and which ones would have to wait. She pondered the question for a while, then decided the ones who'd have a harder time getting adopted would be the ones to go first. That way they'd have more opportunities to find a home.

The sun had just begun to make its appearance when she'd left home. It was a bright ball of light shining against the clear blue sky by the time she reached the farm. She parked and looked around. Cade's truck was nowhere to be seen. Megan called a cheery good morning to the animals as she stepped into the barn. The dogs barked and put their paws on the doors of their stalls, so she let them into the corral, where they immediately began to run around and sniff the ground.

She had cleaned the litter boxes and was filling the food bowls when she heard Cade's truck pull up. He walked into the barn a minute later.

"Well, this is a surprise," he said.

"A pleasant one, I hope."

"Definitely. I didn't expect to see you here so early."

"It's Saturday, which means I don't have to work, so I can take care of my responsibilities here."

"You know I don't mind handling morning duty."

"I came for a second reason. Rebekah has space for

two cats and one dog at the shelter. I plan on dropping them off later this morning."

"Do you know which ones?"

"I think Bella and Felix for the cats."

"The two troublemakers?"

Megan nodded.

"And the dog?"

"I don't know. Maybe Pee-Wee."

Cade nodded. "That sounds like a good idea."

Once the animals were fed, Cade turned to her. "What do you plan to do for the rest of the day? Besides stop by the shelter."

"Nothing. I figured I play it by ear."

"Do you want to spend some time here? Get a taste of real farm life?"

"I'd love it. If you don't think I'll be in the way."

"Not at all. Come on."

Before they went anywhere, they said good morning to Reginald. He poured them each a cup of coffee, and they talked while he cooked breakfast. Although Megan had eaten a bowl of cereal before she'd driven to the farm, she found she had room for the French toast, sausage and scrambled eggs Reginald made.

Reginald and Cade kidded each other throughout breakfast while Megan watched in amusement. There was something so sweet about the way Cade and his dad got along. It was easy to tell how much they enjoyed spending time together. Listening to the affectionate tone in Cade's voice as he spoke to his father only made him more attractive to her.

So many people their age didn't appreciate their parents and didn't include them in their lives. It did her heart good to see how much Cade loved his father and the large part they played in each other's lives.

After they'd finished eating, Megan offered to help with the dishes, but Reginald shooed her away. "It's much too nice a day for you to spend it inside. Besides, I have a system."

"Thank you for a delicious breakfast."

"Anytime, Megan. Anytime."

Megan wanted to believe that she truly was welcome anytime, but despite the joy filling her heart at his words, the experience with Tim's family left her wary. Could she trust that his affection for her would remain even after the animals no longer needed to stay on his farm or would it vanish like mist when the sun rose? Though unsure if Reginald's affection would last, Megan kissed his cheek, then followed Cade from the kitchen.

Megan played close attention as Cade showed her around the farm. There was so much to see and she didn't want to miss a single detail. Up close, the endless rows of plants looked like a piece of art. The tomato plants were pretty enough to be used as landscaping. After walking among the growing vegetables, Cade drove along a dirt road for about twenty minutes. When he stopped, they were on a small hill. After they climbed from the truck, Megan walked around. Almost immediately she spotted a herd of cows. From this vantage point they looked smaller than they actually were.

She turned to Cade, who was looking into the valley, a proud look on his face. "How many are there?"

"Thirty-five hundred."

"That's a lot."

"Yes."

"I've been thinking. I don't want to interfere with your plans for your business, but I wonder if you've talked to Amanda Sylvester."

The Sylvesters were a fixture in town thanks to their long-established restaurant, Main Street Grille. Amanda had managed the restaurant and run the kitchen capably for years but—as Megan had learned after befriending the cheerful brunette—she was in the process of starting a new business.

"About what?"

"She's no longer running her family's restaurant. She's starting her own catering business. I think she's the kind of client you're looking for."

"That sounds promising. I'll contact her and see what we can work out. Thank you for thinking of me."

"You're both good people who want to provide the best for your customers. A partnership between you can't help but be a success."

Cade smiled, obviously pleased by her response, and they continued touring the farm. With every step she took, Megan felt more comfortable, both on the farm and with Cade.

When Cade had shown her everything, they returned to the barn. Megan was sorry to see the pleasant morning come to an end, but he had work to do and she needed to deliver the animals to the shelter. They crated the cats and Pee-Wee and put the carriers into the back seat of her car. She touched Cade's hand. "Thanks so much for showing me around. I really enjoyed myself. I'll be back in time to feed the rest of the gang tonight."

"That's a lot of driving back and forth in one day."

"I don't mind."

"In that case, I'll see you later." Cade held the car door open for her, then closed it firmly after she'd gotten inside.

Megan glanced in her rearview mirror as she drove away. Cade was still standing there, watching her leave. She wondered if he was going to miss her while she was gone. Since she was already missing him, she hoped so.

She told herself to snap out of it. She'd rushed headlong into a relationship before and gotten hurt. There was no way she was going to make that mistake again. Besides, Cade was her client, and business and pleasure didn't mix. Of course she was probably getting concerned over nothing. Although he'd become much more pleasant, Cade hadn't shown the slightest interest in a romantic relationship. Heck, they were barely friends.

As she drove to the shelter, she couldn't help comparing her growing feelings for Cade with her ex, Tim, and she was coming to realize that Tim had been right to end their relationship. They hadn't been in love for a while. And with time to think as well as her reaction to Cade, Megan wondered if she'd ever been in love with him. She'd liked and admired Tim. He was one of the good guys. And they'd always had a good time together. But the truth was she probably wouldn't have wanted to marry him if not for his family. She'd loved them all. More than that, she'd loved being part of a family again. Looking back, she knew that hadn't been fair to Tim, who'd deserved better.

Five minutes later, she reached the shelter and pulled into the parking lot. Since it was Saturday there were several people milling around. Some were volunteers, but most were families in search of a pet to call their own. Megan hoped that someone would want each of the animals she was dropping off. She whispered a prayer that whoever chose these pets would treat them with the utmost love and kindness.

Megan opened the door and pulled out the two cat carriers. She was reaching for the dog's leash when Birdie spotted her and rushed over to help. Megan smiled at the other woman. "Thanks."

"Anytime." Birdie looked into the cat crates. "And who do you have here?"

"That's Bella and Felix. And this little fellow is Pee-Wee."

"Welcome, friends." Birdie straightened and then looked at Megan. "I imagine you're wondering if Bunny and I have reached a decision about whether we want to bring charges against Gator."

Megan hadn't planned on mentioning it, but since Birdie was the one to bring it up, Megan didn't see a problem with having the conversation. "Have you?"

"Not yet. It's just so hard to think about prosecuting our brother and possibly sending him to jail. He's our flesh and blood. Family."

"Nobody knows how important family is more than I do. But he embezzled money from you. I've already told you what I think you should do, and I won't badger either of you. But I want to tell you one more thing. Don't put more value on family ties than he does."

"He's our brother."

"I know. And he was your brother when he stole from you."

Birdie nodded and Megan hoped she'd gotten through to her. Megan liked both of the Whitaker sisters and hated to see someone take advantage of them.

Megan and Birdie took the animals inside, and a sweet faced volunteer got them set up for what Megan hoped would be a very short stay. She'd heard most of the animals were adopted quickly and hoped that would be the case for the sixteen under her care. They deserved homes and families. Love.

Megan stayed around to talk with a few of the volunteers she recognized from her earlier visits before going home. After taking a long shower, she returned to the farm. When she arrived, she stopped in and said a quick hello to Reginald before going in search of her charges. She spent a good fifteen minutes rubbing the cats and another twenty minutes or so playing fetch with the dogs. After giving them fresh water, she left them to their own devices.

During her search for the cats the other day, she'd seen a pond in the distance and now decided to wander there for a closer look. She'd taken a few steps in that direction when she heard Cade calling her name. She turned and waited for him to catch up to her.

"Hey," she said.

He smiled at her. "Hey yourself. Where are you going?"

"I thought I'd take a walk to the pond near where we found the cats."

"That sounds like a good way to spend the afternoon. Do you want company?"

"I'd love some."

"Hold on a minute and I'll get some bread to feed the geese." He darted up the stairs and into the house. Megan noticed that Cade was wearing a different pair of jeans and another shirt than he'd had on this morning. And his chin looked freshly shaved. His fresh appearance made her doubly glad that she'd taken the time to shower and spritz on perfume before she'd come back.

Cade held up a half loaf of bread as he jogged down the stairs. When he reached her, they turned and walked side by side to the pond. Megan spotted a bunch of wildflowers and stopped to sniff them.

"You can pick some if you want."

"Thanks." She studied them for a second before pulling a couple.

Since they weren't in any particular hurry, Megan stopped every now and then to pick a few flowers. By the time they reached the pond she was holding a colorful bouquet. She set it on the ground while Cade pulled several slices of bread from the plastic wrap. Megan took some and walked to the water's edge. Several geese were floating in the water while others pecked at the grass.

Megan tore the bread into pieces and edged closer.

She dropped a few pieces onto the ground. "Here, goosey-goosey."

The geese turned and honking loudly began to walk in her direction. She dropped a few more pieces of bread and the geese charged her, honking all the while. They came from all directions and suddenly afraid, she threw the last of the bread at them then held up her hands to indicate that she didn't have any more food. The geese didn't understand that signal and kept closing in on her. There had to be at least two or three dozen of them and the circle closed in around her. Megan squealed and, tripping over a couple of the birds, ran away as fast as she could. The geese followed.

Cade was several yards away, tossing bread at the geese in the water, and he turned at her cry. Before he could take more than two steps in her direction, she ran past him and hid behind his back. Hopefully the geese would take one look at Cade and all of his muscles and back off. They didn't. The geese kept coming, clearly determined to get even more bread.

Megan whimpered. What had she started?

Cade chuckled then set her away from him. "Don't worry. I'll protect you. Stay right here."

She nodded, but she was still trembling.

Cade walked up to the geese, waving his arms wildly. "Shoo. Shoo. No more food here."

As he drew nearer, still gesturing and talking loudly, the geese turned and began waddling back toward the pond. Finally they all got in the water and began swimming away. Once they'd sailed across the water, Cade smiled and walked to Megan.

"My hero." She put her hands around his waist and hugged him tight, then reached up and kissed his cheek. She'd intended to keep things light, but when her lips touched his warm skin, electricity shot through her body, stunning her with its intensity. It was like grabbing a live wire. She sucked in a breath and got a whiff of his heady scent mingled with a hint of aftershave. He smelled so good. Their eyes met and held, and sexual attraction arced between them.

He wrapped his arms around her waist and pulled her closer to him. She leaned her head against his chest, feeling the steady beat of his heart beneath his cotton shirt. It felt so good to be in his embrace. She couldn't imagine anything would ever feel better. They stood that way for a long moment before Cade eased back and set her away from him. Megan wasn't sure what had gone wrong. Could she have imagined the heat in his eyes or the way his breath had hitched when she'd kissed him?

She didn't think so. She knew he felt the same longing she had. But he kept his distance from her as they returned to the barn, and doubts began to take hold. Perhaps she'd imagined his reaction, seeing what she'd wanted to see. She'd been rejected before and didn't want to feel that sting again. There was no way she would put herself on the spot by asking why he'd suddenly become cold. She might not like the answer. And since she'd be coming to Battle Lands Farm to care for the animals for the foreseeable future, it would be best not to open that can of worms. Besides, he was her client and off-limits. She needed to remember that.

* * *

Megan didn't say much as they fed the animals and that was fine with Cade. With all the noise and confusion suddenly filling his head he wouldn't have been able to form a coherent thought much less carry on an intelligent conversation. Sometimes it was best to be quiet rather than risk saying the wrong thing. In this case the wrong thing would be to ask Megan to come with him into town for dinner and a movie. Or maybe for a walk around the farm. He wanted her company for a few more hours. Or maybe for the night. Thoughts like that would lead him down a path he shouldn't travel, so it was best to keep his mouth shut.

Megan was a city girl. And not just any city girl. She was a lawyer from New York City. That was two strikes against any relationship he and Megan could ever have. His former fiancée had ended their engagement a few weeks before the wedding day, then run away to Chicago with her lawyer boyfriend. Cade knew that some people might believe he was being irrational to group all city girls into the same category, or to feel a grudge against lawyers, but he knew he was just being practical.

Life on a farm could be lonely and isolated. His former fiancée, Deadra, had sworn she'd be happy living on his piece of land. She'd claimed that she could be happy anywhere as long as they were together. That all she'd needed was him. He'd believed her. Once the reality of living in his house had set in, she'd dumped him and returned to big city life where she'd been happy.

He'd grown up here and liked his life on the farm.

The quiet solitude didn't bother him. Though she seemed content now, Cade believed in his heart that that Megan wouldn't be able to adjust to life here any better than Deadra had. It would be foolhardy to think otherwise.

Megan had been in the area for a couple of months. The time she'd spent in Spring Forest could be likened to a long vacation. People visited places that were different from their normal lives in order to have new experiences. A small North Carolina town was definitely a novelty for her. No doubt she enjoyed spending time in such a charming town. But eventually she would get tired of the slower pace and crave the activity of New York once more. When that happened she'd be gone and Cade would be left behind. He would be a fool to open himself up to someone who was so wrong for him—especially a woman like Megan who made his heart skip a beat every time he saw her. It would be way too easy to get in over his head with her, if he let himself. But he wouldn't. He'd been a fool once. He wasn't going to make that mistake again.

That's why he needed to keep her at a distance.

Chapter Eight

The next couple of days, Cade struggled to keep his attraction under control. The frustrating thing was no matter how much your head knew something was bad for you, it was nearly impossible to convince your heart. Not that his heart was what he was worried about. There was no way he could be falling in love with Megan at this stage in the game. He barely knew her. Right now he was in what could only be described as a serious state of attraction, and if he wasn't careful, his body would get him into trouble.

She was just so beautiful. So witty and fun. Last night his father had invited Megan to stay for dinner and she'd said yes instantly. Though Cade should know better, he'd been glad when she'd agreed to stay. She hadn't stayed for dinner since the day they'd walked to the pond. Instead she took care of the pets every evening and then left. Since he'd made up his mind to keep his distance, he should be glad, but he wasn't. He missed her.

Reginald never let anyone touch his stove, but he'd accepted Megan's offer of assistance and let her make the gravy. That might not be a big deal to anyone else, but for Reginald it was like giving her a house key.

Dinner had been fun with Megan joining in the conversation. It had felt so right having her there. It was as if she was a member of the family. And though he knew he was getting ahead of himself, there had been a couple of times he'd actually pictured her there permanently. Maybe he'd been wrong to judge her based upon where she'd been born and raised. People couldn't control their place of birth. And who was he to judge someone based upon their career?

He'd encountered many people who'd talked down to him, assuming that because he was a farmer he was uneducated. It wasn't true, of course. He had an education. He'd chosen to be a farmer because he enjoyed it. He hadn't felt compelled to change his career because of what someone else thought of him. It was just as wrong to make assumptions about Megan simply because she'd chosen to become a lawyer.

Cade closed the accounting book and slid it into the center desk drawer. They were still operating on budget, which always put Cade in a good mood. He glanced at his watch and stood. It was almost time for Megan to arrive. After taking a quick shower, he drove to the barn. He stepped inside just as Megan finished pouring food into the bowls. The number of animals staying on the farm was dwindling. Two more dogs had been dropped off at the shelter a couple of days ago. Bella, Felix and Pee-Wee had already been adopted. Megan's eyes had filled with tears when she'd told him they had been rehomed. She should have been happy, but they hadn't been tears of joy. It had taken him a minute to figure out why. Though she was glad the animals had found families, she was sad to know that she probably wouldn't see them again. She loved them and now they were lost to her.

"Hey." Megan smiled as he walked into the barn. As usual, she was friendly, although she hadn't touched him again.

"Hi. How was your day?"

"Great. How about yours?"

"Busy." The conversation should have been mundane, and it would have been had he been talking to anyone other than Megan. Nothing was dull if it involved her. The only thing that mattered was her presence. Being with her eased the loneliness that had consumed him for a long time. Spending time with Megan at the end of the day felt right, and despite himself, he'd begun to imagine what his life would be like if she came home to the farm and him every day. He told himself to knock it off, but he was fighting a losing battle. He liked Megan.

When they finished with the dogs, they went into his father's house. As usual, Reginald was in the kitchen. He looked up and smiled. "Well, if it isn't my sous chef."

Megan saluted. "At your service."

"Well, I don't need your help tonight. I have it all

handled. As a matter of fact, I'll have dinner on the table in five minutes, so go wash your hands. Both of you."

Cade and Megan walked side by side to the powder room. The heat from her body gently caressed his, awakening his desire. There was something intimate about sharing soap and then rinsing their hands at the same time. He was standing so near to her that he inhaled the fragrance of her shampoo with each breath.

Reginald was setting a basket of homemade rolls on the table as Megan and Cade returned to the kitchen. Cade pulled out Megan's chair and then sat down across from her. As usual, the conversation was lively, and Megan told a funny story or two. After dinner, Reginald stood. "I hate to eat and run, but my favorite program is coming on in about ten minutes, so I'm going to leave you good people now."

"Would you like to go for a walk, or have you had enough of the outside for the day?" Cade asked Megan when they were alone.

"I work in an office. You're the one who spent the day outside, so the question is, have you had enough?"

He extended a hand. She took it and they walked outside. Her palm was so soft and warm, especially against his callused one.

The weather was pleasant and a cool breeze blew. The sun was beginning to set and birds were chirping in the trees. He wanted to show her more of his farm. There was so much to see, but rather than choose which direction they went, he asked her preference.

"You know what I'd really like to do?" she asked. Her voice sounded tentative, almost sheepish.

He smiled to encourage her. "What?"

"I'd like to walk down the driveway until we reach the glider. Then I'd like to just sit and swing."

"We can do that."

"It is so peaceful here," Megan said as they strolled through the silent night.

"I thought it might be too slow for you."

"Because I'm from New York?"

"Yes."

"Believe it or not, New Yorkers actually enjoy quiet moments. Just because there's something to do just about every hour of every day doesn't mean we actually do everything. Sure, I liked going to plays and concerts, but I also enjoyed sitting on my couch and reading in the evenings."

"I guess I'm guilty of stereotyping."

She nodded.

They reached the glider and sat down. When his mother had been alive, she and his father had spent many warm evenings sitting on the glider, watching as the stars came out. Since her death, no one sat here. As he set the swing in motion, it occurred to Cade that not enjoying it had been a mistake. That was not the way to honor his mother. She wouldn't have wanted somewhere she found pleasure to sit unused and unloved. This place, filled with memories of his mother, was the perfect place to get to know Megan better.

He glanced over at her. She'd closed her eyes and was leaning against the back of the swing. "Would you tell me more about yourself? I feel like I know the outlines of your life, but I'd like to fill in the details if that's okay with you."

Megan nodded, then sat up and blew out a long breath. She turned and looked at him. "I had the best family. My mom and dad were great and I had a super big brother. My earliest memory is of my mom polishing my toenails red. Mom was really glamorous. She was always dressed in the most beautiful clothes and she never had a hair out of place. Her nails were never chipped. Her makeup was impeccable. She was so gorgeous. She even looked good when she cleaned the house. I wanted to be just like her."

She raised her feet. Although she wore gym shoes, they were coordinated to match her shirt. He didn't doubt that she had a perfect pedicure to match her manicure. Now that he understood why it mattered so much to her, he regretted judging her based on her appearance.

"My dad called me his princess. When I was little, I would look out the window and wait for him to come home from work. The second he walked in the door I'd run to him and he'd pick me up and carry me on his shoulders. It felt so good to be taller than everyone else in the house. Even better was how good it felt to have my Daddy carry me. When I got older and was too big for him to put on his shoulders, I still waited for him to come home.

"Marlon, my big brother, was so smart. He was the best baseball player I've ever seen. He was the star of the high school team and wanted to play in college. Siblings often don't get along, but we did. He was my best friend and I could tell him anything. If I had a problem, he would help me solve it. He always watched out for me no matter what. When I was with him, I knew I was safe.

"Mom and I spent every other Saturday morning together. We'd go shopping or to get our hair and nails done. Then we would go to lunch. At the same time my dad and brother were hanging out and doing what they wanted. The other Saturdays, my dad and I went places and my mom and brother spent the morning together. Dad always found the most fun things to do. We would go to the park and fly kites. Or we would go to a puppet show or matinee. Those days were special. And then they ended."

There were tears running down her face and he wished he had a handkerchief to give her. Since he didn't, he did the next best thing and wiped away her tears with his fingers.

"I'm so sorry that you lost them."

"It's not fair." The softly spoken words were a painful cry from her heart.

"No, it's not."

Still crying, she leaned her head against his chest. He put his arm around her trembling shoulders and held her, offering the only comfort he could. Gradually her tears slowed and she sniffled.

"I didn't mean to make you sad," he apologized. "I shouldn't have asked you to dredge up bad memories."

"The memories weren't bad. They were the best. I just wish I could have had more time with my family."

"So do I." He would give his right arm if it meant

she could still have her family. But life didn't work that way. There was nothing he could do to give her back her parents and brother.

"After the accident, I was alone. Really alone. I already told you that my parents were only children so I didn't have any aunts, uncles or cousins. Unfortunately I didn't have any grandparents either. My mother's parents had been really old when they'd had her and they died when I was little. I don't remember much about them. My father had been raised by a single mother and she'd died of cancer before I was born. So I ended up in foster care."

He'd heard so many horrible things about foster care that his imagination immediately went into overdrive. "How was that?"

"It wasn't terrible. The people didn't starve or beat me or anything like that, but I never felt at home with any of them. The first family actually sent me back after a few weeks. They said I was difficult and not trying to blend in. Remember I had just lost my entire family. I was in shock and not ready or able to be a part of someone else's family. Not to mention that I had to move from my home and everything that was familiar to me. I even had to change schools.

"The foster families always claimed that they considered me part of the family, but that wasn't how they treated me or the other foster kids. We didn't get the same attention or new clothes or any number of things that their biological kids got."

She sighed and stared at the horizon. He wished he knew what she was thinking. Feeling. "One family used me as their unpaid babysitter. They kept saying they let me watch their four-year-old twins because they trusted me, but really it was because I was free and had no choice. As soon as the kids started kindergarten, they sent me back. They didn't need me anymore. I lived with another foster family until the wife found out she was pregnant. They sent me back, too. They didn't need a pretend daughter anymore because they were about to have their own kid."

His heart ached for the way she'd been treated. His hand fisted in anger. "I'm sorry."

"I survived. For a while I tried to fit in, but after a while I knew it was futile. I'd had one family and I'd lost them. I wasn't going to get another." She paused and the finality of her words hit him in the gut.

"Once I turned eighteen, I went to college and then law school. I was able to have my own place where I could cook what I wanted, watch what I wanted on television and buy quality clothes. Clothes my mother would have helped me pick out on our Saturday mornings together if she'd still been alive.

"When I went into foster care, one of my father's friends rented a storage unit for me so I was able to keep some of my parents' things. Not much—the unit wasn't that big. But I was able to hold on to a couple pieces of furniture and some of their favorite works of art. Some photo albums and some of my mother's favorite jewelry and dresses. Mr. Wilson paid the fee every month until I was able to. When I got my first apartment I filled it with my memories. It was almost like getting part of my family back."

He didn't know what to say, so he didn't say a word.

"You pretty much know the rest. I worked for a while and then I moved to North Carolina."

"I'm very glad you did." He was becoming happier about that with each passing day.

As they sat there together, Cade realized that something he'd once believed was impossible was happening. He was falling for Megan. She was sweeter than he'd imagined. But letting his feelings for her continue to grow would be a mistake of colossal proportions. It would be one thing to fall for her if he actually believed she would stay in town. But he didn't. The wise thing to do would be to keep her at a distance and protect his heart.

Megan couldn't believe she'd told Cade so much about herself. She never revealed the details about her past to anyone. Sure, she'd spoken about her family and time in foster care in general terms, but never with the emotion that she'd let flow from her today. And the tears. She never cried. At least not where anyone could see her. Yet just now with Cade, her guard had come tumbling down, and when the words had fallen from her mouth she'd been unable to stop them. She'd revealed too much of herself. Though she tried to hold it back, a stray tear slipped from her eye and she attempted to wipe it away before he noticed.

She sneaked a look at Cade. He was staring into space as if digesting what he'd heard. Would knowing the details of her life change his impression of her? Some people looked down on foster children as if the fact that they had spent time being raised by other people made them defective. Undesirable. As if it was their fault their families had died. He hadn't seemed to react that way, but it was impossible to know what another person felt unless they told you.

She'd shared so much about herself. It was only fair that he do the same. Knowing more about him would help her to feel less vulnerable. "I just told you about my life. Do you mind telling me about yours? I know you have a brother named Chase, but all I know about him is his name. Is he older? Younger? Married? Single? Do you guys get along?"

"All of these questions about Chase. Should I be worried?"

What did that mean? Did it mean that he was considering them as more than friends? Was he hinting that he had romantic interest in her? Or was she reading more into the statement than he meant? "Nope. I just want to know more about you. Learning about your family is one way to do that."

"I know. I was just kidding. Chase is two years older than I am. And just like you and your brother, we get along well. We're pretty good friends although we don't see each other as often as I'd like since he lives in Raleigh and I live here. Even so, we talk all the time and get together for dinner or just to hang out a couple times a month."

"Okay." Megan looked at Cade. He looked so calm. One of the things she admired about him was his confidence and self-assurance. "What about you? I know your father is transferring ownership of the farm to you and Chase. Have you always wanted to run the farm, or did you want to go somewhere else and see the rest of the world?"

He gave her an odd look and stiffened just the tiniest bit. She wouldn't have noticed if she hadn't been leaning against him. Why had he reacted that way to a perfectly normal question?

"I did leave the farm. I got a degree in agricultural science from North Carolina State University in Raleigh. I liked college and enjoyed the time I lived in Raleigh, but I always intended to return to the farm. Battle Lands has been in my family for generations. I feel a connection to my ancestors in every acre."

Megan sighed. She'd give anything to have someplace in the world where she knew without a doubt that she belonged. A place with a connection so deep that she could reach back and touch the people who'd come before her. Instead she was rootless. For the past fourteen years life had been a strong wind, blowing her from pillar to post. She longed for good soil like here on Cade's farm where she could sink in and grow roots. If she ever found such a place she'd be able to flourish with the knowledge that she was wanted and that she actually had a place to call home.

She liked the little house she was renting. It was charming and cozy and she felt at peace there. But still, she longed for a home filled with laughter like the one where she'd lived for the first fourteen years of her life. A home filled with people who cared for and supported each other. She wanted a husband and kids she could love with her whole heart and who would love her the same way in return. Over the years she'd made good friends, but friends, no matter how close, didn't fill the empty place in her heart that craved a family.

Once more she glanced at Cade. Could he be a part of that family? Could she find a forever home with him on the Battle Lands Farm? More and more she was starting to wonder if she'd finally found a place to belong, and the hope she'd thought had died began to grow.

But then reality set in. This farm wasn't her home any more than any of the foster homes had been. To hope or dream otherwise was only setting herself up for more pain.

They sat in silence for a while. As it grew later, the moon was joined in the sky by hundreds of bright stars. Cade covered a yawn and she knew it was time to leave. "I guess I had better get a move on. I don't want to overstay my welcome."

Cade stood and helped her get to her feet. "It is getting pretty late. We'd better get you back to your car."

She'd hoped he'd say something about how she was always welcome, but he didn't. Although he'd held her hand when they'd walked out here earlier, once she was standing, he let go of her hand and shoved his into the pocket of his jeans.

Had she said something wrong? She replayed the conversation. Nothing stood out. She hadn't insulted him or been rude. Once more she questioned the wisdom of revealing so much of herself to him. Perhaps she should have done what she usually did and glossed over her time in foster care and focused on her life after college and law school. Still, she didn't regret telling him the truth. She wasn't ashamed of her past. If he couldn't handle knowing, that was his shortcoming, not hers.

When they reached her car, he held the door for her as he always did. "Call me when you get home so I'll know you arrived safely."

"I will." She looked out the rearview mirror and saw him standing there. What she wouldn't give to be standing there beside him.

Chapter Nine

Cade watched until he could no longer see the tail-lights on Megan's car, then went to check on the animals. The cats had settled into their preferred beds in their cat mansions, minus Samson, who was hanging out with Delilah. The dogs were lying around in the corral, their chew toys and balls ignored. When they saw him they jumped to their feet and ran over. Apparently they were ready to go to bed.

Once they were settled, he went into his father's house. His dad was sitting at the table with a book in his hands. When Cade walked in, Reginald looked up. If he was surprised to see Cade, he didn't show it.

His father had cleaned the kitchen and set the pots he'd planned to use to cook breakfast on the stove. A pot of coffee was brewing and Reginald grabbed two mugs from the cabinet and handed one to Cade. Neither Cade nor his father would be affected by drinking caffeine this late at night. As hard as they worked, they'd be asleep within minutes of putting their heads on their pillows.

"So, I take it Megan's gone."

Cade nodded.

"How do you feel about that?"

Trust his dad to get to the point. But then, it was late, and they didn't have time to waste dancing around. Of course Cade wouldn't go to sleep until he'd heard from Megan. The drive from the farm to Spring Forest was safe and he didn't expect anything untoward to happen to her. But accidents happened. Cars got flat tires. Deer ran into the road. Drunks got behind the wheel when they shouldn't. The caffeine might not keep him awake, but worry would.

"How should I feel? She took care of the animals just as she said she would. She's holding up her end of the bargain."

"I bet that surprised the heck out of you. I could tell you expected her to stop coming or slack off."

"I did. She didn't look like someone who would actually do the work."

"She may be a city girl, but she's not Deadra. Just because she wears fancy clothes and jewelry doesn't mean she thinks she's too good to work on a farm. I talked to her many times and didn't once hear her complain about the dirt or cleaning up after animals. And she didn't whine about breaking a nail."

"That's because she didn't break a nail."

Reginald frowned. "Don't be dense. You know what I mean."

Yes, Cade did know what his father meant. He also knew that just because Megan didn't complain didn't mean she didn't look down her pretty little nose on farmers and the work they did. Just because she was too polite to say it didn't mean she wasn't thinking it. More than likely it was simply a result of the life she'd lived. She'd had to try and fit in to so many places and with so many families that he doubted she would ever verbally express dissatisfaction with anything. He wondered if she ever said what she actually felt. Did she ever relax and just be herself? Or was she always playing a role, trying to be whatever her audience wanted her to be?

Not that he would blame her if she did. He'd always had a place to belong and had always known he was loved, so he'd been free to be as negative and unpleasant as he wanted without fear of being sent away. She hadn't had that privilege. He rubbed a hand down his face. They were so different. They'd lived entirely different lives. There were depths and complexities to her he didn't understand. Maybe he never would. Still, he was willing to try.

It was possible Megan found him just as confusing as he found her. Although he thought of himself as a simple farmer, he was the first to admit that he'd changed since Deadra had run off. Before then he'd been a people person. He wouldn't describe himself as having been the life of the party, but at least he'd attended parties and socialized with his friends. Now the last thing he wanted was to be around a bunch of people. He was happy with his own company. And though he liked Megan and occasionally allowed himself to imagine what life would be like if she was around and living on the farm, he wouldn't let that thought take root. Maybe if he'd met her before he'd met Deadra. But he hadn't. He was different now and unwilling to take a chance.

"So she doesn't come right out and say that she looks down on farmers. Am I supposed to give her special points for that?" Cade asked, suddenly feeling angry even though he knew he was being unreasonable.

"Are we evaluating Megan now? And for what position?" Reginald looked pointedly at Cade and he squirmed.

"No position. There are no vacancies." He looked into his coffee cup. Nothing remained but the dregs. "I've got to go. I'll see you in the morning."

"Keep running for a while longer if that makes you feel better."

"I'm not running. I simply refuse to make a fool of myself again over the wrong woman." Megan might be in Spring Forest now, but she wouldn't stay. It was obvious that she was looking for something. When she discovered that it wasn't here, she would go back to New York or on to the next place and continue her search. Whatever it was she was looking for, she'd made it clear that it wasn't him. She might not have said the words directly, but her asking if he ever wanted to see more of the world left no doubt that she thought he should want more than to run his family farm.

She wanted him to want more. To be more, just as Deadra had. Megan had seemed surprised that he had a college degree and that he'd actually left the farm for four years to get it.

Deadra had tried to convince him that there was more to life than being a farmer. He'd known that. He'd graduated at the top of his college class. He could have gone anywhere and done anything he wanted. What he'd wanted was to run Battle Lands Farm and to get his farm-to-table business established. That hadn't been enough for Deadra and he doubted it would be for Megan. Megan might surprise him if he'd give her the opportunity. But he wasn't in the mood for taking chances with his heart. Not again, when the devastating results were predictable.

He stopped at the barn before he drove to his house. As expected, Samson and Delilah were waiting for him, so he let them out of their stall, and they followed him to his truck. He was closing the door when his cell phone rang. He glanced at the screen. Megan. Despite knowing that she was totally wrong for him, his heart skipped a beat as he pressed the button to talk.

"I'm home," she said as soon as he'd answered.

Although that was all he needed to know, he got out of the car and leaned against the hood, leaving the door open in case Samson or Delilah wanted to get out. They glanced at him and then lay down on the seat, making their decision clear. "How was the ride?"

"Uneventful, which is just the way I like it."

Smiling, he shook his head at her comment. He could hear her moving around and wondered if she was getting ready for bed. The thought of her undressing popped into his head, filling his imagination with images he couldn't get rid of no matter how hard he tried. He realized he hadn't replied to her so he said the first thing that came to his mind. "Good."

"I'll be there same time tomorrow, if that's okay with you."

"That's fine." He checked his watch. He'd see her again in less than twelve hours.

"Then I'll say goodnight. Have sweet dreams."

"You, too." He didn't know whether his dreams would be sweet, but he knew that she would be starring in them.

Cade stepped into the building housing the Sutton Law Offices, then crossed the simply decorated reception area and smiled at the receptionist.

She returned his smile. "How can I help you?"

"I'm Cade Battle. I have an appointment with Megan Jennings."

"Of course." She checked something on her computer and then picked up her phone. A few moments later she spoke again, presumably to Megan. "Mr. Battle is here to see you. Will do." She hung up and stood. "Follow me, please."

They walked down a hallway, stopping at a closed door. The receptionist knocked once before she opened the door and stepped aside, letting him enter.

"Thanks, Emma," Megan said as she crossed the room. "Come on in, Cade. I have the contracts all set for you. Let's sit down and go through them."

Megan was dressed in a red skirt that skimmed her curves and stopped just above her knees. A matching jacket hung on the back of the door. Although the suit was professional, it didn't disguise her curvaceous body. He realized he was staring and quickly replayed her comment so that he could respond intelligently. He was turning into the bumbling farmer stereotype he hated. "That sounds good."

There were two chairs in front of her desk and she indicated for him to take one. He'd expected her to return to her seat behind the desk, but she surprised him by sitting beside him. Her sweet perfume filled his nostrils and it took all of his control not to lean in closer and inhale deeply. This was a business meeting, not a date. They were in her office, for goodness sake. Besides, hadn't he decided that they were wrong for each other? That he wasn't going to make a fool of himself over her? Well, if wanting to slide his hand under her glorious hair and sniff her neck didn't make him a fool, he didn't know what did.

While he'd been consumed with thoughts of her, Megan had grabbed a folder from her desk and pulled a stack of papers from it. "There are two documents in here. The first one is the article of incorporation creating your company. I've already filed everything with the secretary of state and paid the required fee."

She'd already explained the procedure to him and reviewed each step thoroughly when he'd authorized her to take these steps, so he flipped through the pages and nodded.

"This other document is the contract you'll use with your clients. Everything is spelled out clearly. I've left blank spaces so you can specify what you will provide, when, and the price." She pointed out the spaces as she talked, and he couldn't help but notice her perfectly shaped nails were the exact same shade of red as her skirt and shoes. He recalled how her voice had been filled with awe and a bit of pain as she told him how her mother had polished her nails. He wondered if this was the color red from that memory.

She looked up and when their eyes locked, he realized he'd been lost in his train of thought. Her eyes were so beautiful, and for a moment all he wanted to do was stare into them for the rest of the day. But he couldn't. They had business to handle.

He needed to keep his focus on what was important to him, and that was getting his business up and running. This was a good start, but it was only a start. He picked up the contract and read through it. It contained everything he'd asked for as well as some legal protections he hadn't considered but that Megan had said were essential. "This is perfect. Thank you."

A shadow crossed her face before her expression became neutral, but he'd seen it. Despite the approving words, his tone had been more abrupt than he'd intended—he hadn't meant to sound abrupt at all—and he instantly regretted it. Protecting his heart was essential, but not at the expense of hers. Her heart had been hurt enough.

She stacked the papers and slid them into the folder, which she handed to him. "I've emailed you the contract so you can print it off as you need it, but I've also printed off several copies to get you started."

"Thank you."

Instead of standing and ending the meeting, she

looked at him. "Are we okay? You seem distant. If I did or said anything to offend you, I'm sorry."

"You didn't. We're still friends. If I'm preoccupied, it's because I'm excited about getting started. I'm meeting with Amanda in a little while. If all goes well, I'll be a supplier for her new catering business." He stood. "As a matter of fact, I need to get going. I don't want to be late for my first business meeting with my very first client."

Megan stood, as well. The heat from her body reached out and surrounded him, tempting him to wrap her in his arms and kiss her the way he'd wanted to since he'd walked into the office. But he wouldn't. Kissing her would allow his feelings to grow. Once that happened, it would only be a matter of time before he was in love with her. Then where would he be?

She must have had the same thought, because she gave him a smile that didn't come anywhere near to reaching her eyes as she stepped back and went around to her side of the desk. He'd blown it. Even if he wanted to, there would be no going back. Still, he didn't want to end things this way. Not that they were ending. They still had animals on the farm for her to feed. True, another three had been moved to the shelter and would more than likely be adopted soon, but that still left nine animals for her to care for.

"Good luck with your meeting. Amanda is a good person and I'm sure you'll enjoy doing business with her. I wish both of you much success."

He nodded and held out his hand in a move that he knew was too formal given how close they'd become, but it was too late to pull it back. That would only hurt her feelings more. She took his hand and gave a firm shake.

Cade tapped the folder containing the documents that were the first step in his successful future on Megan's desk, then tucked it under his arm before leaving her office. As he walked out of the firm and drove to his meeting with Amanda, he wondered if there would be a way to undo the damage he'd just done.

Megan managed to keep her smile in place until she was sure Cade had left the office. Once she heard the roar of his truck engine grow faint as he drove down the road, she sank into her chair. Tears threatened, but she held them at bay. The office was no place for crying. If she broke down, she'd lose the respect of her co-workers. She'd already lost too much in her lifetime. There was no way she would voluntarily lose more.

She straightened her clothes and went into the reception area. She'd skipped lunch and decided to go out for a bite. Emma was sitting at her desk, getting ready to leave. Emma had placed several pictures on her desk of her soon-to-be-stepdaughters holding kittens, and Megan leaned in for a closer look. "The girls are adorable. And so are the kittens."

Emma smiled. "Aren't they though?"

Megan stared at one of the pictures. The fluffy black kitten looked so much like Samson. Of course, he'd only recently been neutered, so who knew, perhaps they were related. Sure, there were lots of black cats in the world—but she liked the idea of thinking that Samson had family and that he wasn't all alone in the world. Everyone needed family.

She just wished she had one.

Chapter Ten

"I hope I'm not too early," Cade said when the front door of Amanda's house swung open.

"Of course not." Amanda gestured for him to step inside. "I'm so excited about what we are about to do. I've dreamed of having a catering business of my own for a long time, and now it's becoming a reality."

"That's exactly how I feel about the farm-to-table business, and that's why we are going to become such a huge success." Cade found himself echoing Megan's enthusiasm.

Amanda held up her hands. She'd crossed her fingers as if hoping for good luck. He laughed although he was not opposed to good luck. Heck, he'd cross his fingers, too, if he thought it would work. But he knew the only thing they could count on to make them successful was hard work. He was willing to work as hard and as long as necessary to make his dream a reality.

"Have you met my fiancé?" she asked, leading him further into the house.

"I don't believe so."

A man stood as they reached the dining room. He extended his hand. "Ryan Carter. And this is my son, Dillon."

A boy of about six was rolling around the floor with a little dog. The boy looked up and smiled before resuming his game.

"Dillon loves that dog and never goes anywhere without him," Ryan said. "They're best buds."

Cade thought of Delilah and his growing attachment to the dog and could totally relate. He didn't want to think of the day when it would no longer be necessary for Delilah to live on the farm. He knew she needed a forever home and the right thing to do was to help her find one, but sometimes it felt like she belonged with him. He was tempted to try to adopt her himself…but he was pressed for time right now and would become a lot busier once his business was up and running. There wouldn't be enough time to care for a dog then. It would be unfair to keep Delilah if he couldn't give her all the love and affection she deserved. He hoped he was strong enough to let her go when the time came.

"A boy needs a dog," Cade said.

"This boy definitely does," Ryan agreed. He nudged his son with the toe of his shoe. His son stood up and walked from the room. "I know you guys need to get to business, so Dillon and I are going to get out of your hair. Nice meeting you, Cade."

Amanda smiled as she watched her fiancé and his son leave the room, and Cade suddenly found himself wishing he had someone in his life who loved him that way. More than that, he wished there was someone who made him smile the way Amanda and Ryan smiled at each other. Megan's image flashed through his mind and for a minute he imagined her in that role. She was so sweet and kind and seemed to love the farm. But then, she hadn't been in town long. He just couldn't help but think she'd grow tired of living in such a small town. True, they weren't far from Raleigh, but that city in no way compared to New York. No, it was better to think of her as simply a friend. That way neither of them would get hurt.

"Do you have the contract for me to sign?" Amanda asked.

"I do." Cade shifted into business mode. Daydreaming about Megan was dangerous enough when he was alone in his house at night. It would be fatal to his business if he didn't get his head screwed on right.

They sat at the dining room table and read over the contract. Megan hadn't included legal gibberish, so the terms were straightforward and left no room for misunderstandings to arise later. They talked about Amanda's upcoming catering job and what she would need to create the items on her menu. Fortunately everything she needed to complete the order would be ripe and available for picking on the date she needed it. Since she was local, he would have the produce picked and cleaned that morning and delivered that afternoon. You couldn't get any fresher than that. The guaranteed freshness of the produce had been one of the things that convinced her to go with him. That and the visit she'd made to the farm a couple of days ago. He'd given her samples of his fruits and vegetables for her to cook at home. That had sealed the deal.

"I've been thinking," Amanda said slowly. "Would it be okay with you if I came back to the farm and took a few pictures? I'd like to put them on my brochures and website so I can show my customers how fresh the ingredients I use actually are."

"Of course. That's a good idea. I think I'll take some of my own for potential clients who aren't able to visit the farm." He mentally added *create brochure and possibly add a video of the farm to his website* to the list of things he needed to do in order to promote his business. He'd known starting a business wasn't going to be easy, but there were things he hadn't even considered like advertising on an almost nonexistent budget.

When he'd decided to start the business, he'd promised himself that it would be able to stand on its own right from the beginning. He wouldn't pull money that they needed to run the farm to get his own private business up and running. He'd been confident that once word got around about his new venture, local restaurants would seek him out. Now, though, he knew that he would have to actively market the business and cultivate relationships. More drains on his time and more reasons he shouldn't be thinking of Megan. Relationships required time, which was something he didn't have right now.

That was one of Deadra's main complaints. She'd

said that he worked too hard and never had time to spend with her. But when they did spend time together doing something she enjoyed, like dining at fancy restaurants or attending parties thrown by one or another of her swanky friends, she'd gotten upset that they couldn't stay until the crack of dawn. She'd refused to understand the life of a farmer. He'd been willing to make sacrifices for her, but she'd been unwilling to reciprocate. She didn't believe in compromise. Since the breakup, he'd realized that they hadn't ever been a good fit. It had been a painful but necessary lesson. City and country just didn't mix.

Once he and Amanda had completed their business and he'd refused her offer to stay for dinner, Cade said goodbye to Ryan and Dillon and then headed for home. It was about time for Megan to arrive. His heart thumped at the thought of seeing her again. She'd looked so sexy in her suit. Where once he'd been turned off by her professional wardrobe, he'd been turned on this afternoon. Of course he knew she wouldn't be wearing the suit when he saw her later. That would be impractical. But she looked sexy in her jeans and tops, too. The truth was, she'd be sexy no matter what she wore.

When he pulled up to the farm, he was surprised that her car wasn't there. He checked his watch. She should have arrived by now. Dread pooled in his stomach. There was only one way from the town to his farm and he'd traveled that road. If her vehicle had broken down he would have passed it, but he hadn't. Still, something could have gone wrong on her drive from her office to her house.

He was pulling out his phone to call her when his father stepped out of the house. Cade hesitated. Maybe he was overreacting. Maybe she'd gotten held up at work again. And really, she wasn't all that late. He was just anxious to see her again.

"How did your meeting go?" Reginald asked.

"Great. I have my first client. My business is official now."

"Glad to hear it. I knew all of your hard work would pay off."

Cade glanced at his watch and then looked around. Something was different. It took a minute for him to figure out what it was. The dogs weren't in the corral. He looked at his father. "Where are the dogs?"

"Megan came by earlier and fed them. They're in the barn now, all settled for the night."

"She didn't stay."

"No. I tried to get her to stay for dinner, but she said she couldn't tonight. It's a shame, too, since I really enjoy her company. I did convince her to take a plate with her, so I know she won't go hungry."

"Did she give you a message for me?"

"No. Was she supposed to?"

"No." Cade shoved his phone into his pocket. He wasn't going to call her now. There wasn't a need. She was fine and dandy.

"I figured you'd said whatever it was you needed to say at your meeting this afternoon. Was I wrong?"

"No. We said everything we needed to say."

"Good. Well, come on in and get some dinner. I made

roast beef that will melt in your mouth, mashed potatoes, and a green salad."

That was one of Cade's favorite meals, but it was
hard to summon up much enthusiasm for dinner. He'd
gotten so used to having Megan around in the evenings,
taking care of the animals and then eating dinner together. It felt strange not having her near. She was becoming very important to him. He had tried to keep
his distance from her, and had even pushed her away.
So why was he disappointed that she'd taken the hint?

He'd told himself that he wouldn't be a fool again by
falling for a city woman, but perhaps he was being a
fool in a different way. What kind of man pushed away
a woman he was attracted to? A woman who clearly
had a kind heart and whose word he could trust? A stupid man, that's who. A man who was afraid to live and
love. Well, Cade Battle had never been afraid of anything and he was done being a fool. He looked at his father. "Do you mind saving me some dinner? I need to
run out for a while."

"Sure." Reginald went back into the house.

Cade jumped into his truck and drove to Spring Forest. Megan had told him where she lived so he had no
trouble finding her house. Her car was parked in the
street, so he pulled behind it and climbed the short flight
of stairs to her front door. She'd put two chairs and a
small table on one side of the porch and a small bench
on the other. Two large potted plants were on either side
of the door. It was quite the homey space and he was
curious to see what the rest of her house looked like.

After he rang the doorbell, he tried to organize his

thoughts. He knew he'd given Megan mixed signals these past few days and had a lot of explaining to do. Hopefully she would be forgiving and willing to start over. And maybe she'd be interested in discovering whether they could be more than friends. He still was not certain she was going to stay in town, but he knew he'd regret not taking the chance.

"Hey, Cade. Is something wrong? Did you have a problem during your meeting with Amanda?"

He looked up at the sound of her voice. When he saw her, it took all of his control not to stare. She'd changed out of the sexy red suit as he'd expected. Instead of the jeans and top that she normally wore to the farm, she had on a floral sundress that bared her shoulders and hit midthigh. She wasn't wearing shoes and her toenails were painted fire-engine red to match her fingernails.

The words she said struck him in the chest. Naturally she'd gone straight to business, assuming that was the only reason he'd be here. He'd taken the personal off the table by the cowardly way he'd treated her. Instead of talking to her, telling her how he felt and sharing his doubts, he'd backed off and left her to guess the reasons why. Disgusted, he shook his head. He'd been such a fool.

"No?" She opened the door. "Come inside and tell me what happened. I'm sure we can find a way to straighten it out."

"What? No. Everything went fine." She was still holding the door, so he stepped inside and followed her into the front room. There wasn't an overhead light, but several floor and table lamps were lit. Framed photographs were scattered over the tables and a portrait hung over the fireplace. There was a paperback book lying on the beige sofa. She swept it up, glanced inside as if checking the page number, then set it on a teak coffee table.

"Have a seat." She gestured vaguely as if giving him the option of sitting on the sofa or one of the two chairs in the cozy room. He chose a comfortable-looking chair and she sat on the sofa. "If everything went okay, then why are you here?"

"I went home and you weren't there."

"I stopped by and took care of the animals. You can ask Reginald, he'll tell you." Her voice sounded defensive as if she expected him to accuse her of lying.

"He told me. He also said that he invited you to stay for dinner but you turned him down. Why didn't you stay?"

She shrugged. "No reason. I've been spending a lot of time on the farm. I just felt like coming home. Don't get me wrong. I love Reginald. I think he's the best. He's not at all like my father in looks or personality, but there's something about your dad that reminds me of mine. But even so, he's not my dad and the farm isn't my home. I don't want to get too attached to either of them."

Her tone was very definitive and her direct words didn't leave room for misinterpretation. But just because her words were true now didn't mean they would always be true. The farm wasn't her home now, but it could be in the future.

"We both like having you there."

"Thanks. I hate to think that I've been forcing my company on reluctant hosts."

"You haven't."

Megan smiled, and for the first time since he'd stepped inside her house she seemed relaxed. That was good because he wanted her to be happy. But it was bad for him because he was just as confused now as he'd been before he'd shown up. And since he wasn't sure about anything, perhaps he shouldn't try and discuss his feelings now.

They talked for a few more minutes, saying nothing of import, before he stood. "It's getting late so I'd better get going. See you tomorrow?"

"Yes."

He walked beside Megan to the door. When they stepped onto the porch, he was tempted to kiss her good-night, which was insane. They hadn't been on a date. When he got in his truck to drive away, he looked at her house. She was still standing there, so he waved before pulling off and driving away.

Megan stood on her porch long after she could no longer hear the sound of Cade's truck engine. She was puzzled as to why he'd stopped by. He hadn't said anything he couldn't have told her the next time they saw each other. Perhaps he wanted to make sure she'd gotten the message. She couldn't have missed it. She was smart enough to know a brush-off when she saw one. And she'd seen one this afternoon. He'd actually shaken her hand.

She'd been hurt and even a bit surprised, although she shouldn't have been. It wasn't the first time she'd been welcomed into a family and then shunted aside when she was no longer needed. She'd done their legal work so he was ready to kick her to the curb. For a while she'd allowed herself to believe that this time she'd be loved and wanted. That she mattered to someone. To Cade. She'd fantasized about being a part of his family. She'd even shared her deepest feelings with him. Then he'd backed away from her so suddenly her head was spinning. She should have known better. No one wanted her for keeps.

Well, there was no changing that. And sadly it wasn't a total shock this time. After all, Tim and his family had tossed her away. Then she'd been devastated. Now she was merely disappointed. She was losing hope that there was a family for her. Not to replace the one she'd lost. No one would ever replace her beloved parents and brother. But she still longed for people who would love her. People who would celebrate her victories and help her get over her failures. People who would turn a house into a home.

That's why she was so determined to find good homes for Mrs. Crockett's animals. Once they'd been loved and had a good home. And just as happened with her, their home and family had been taken away from them. They were all in need of a forever home.

Speaking of home, she grabbed the mail from her coffee table. She'd gotten a letter from her landlord earlier today. He was selling the house and wanted to give her an opportunity to buy it before he put it on the market. She did like the little house. Her furniture fit perfectly. And she liked the neighborhood. It was quiet and within walking distance of the stores where she liked to shop. But there was something about buying the house that seemed so final. It was as if she was giving up on her dream of ever having a family. Buying a house where she would live alone seemed like a lack of faith in the future. Though her hope was waning, it wasn't totally gone.

She knew that idea was totally irrational. Buying a house was a good investment. Why should she continue paying rent to someone else and have nothing to show for it but a stack of receipts when she could make the same payments to herself and end up with a nice piece of real estate? It might make financial sense to buy a house, but she just wasn't sure.

It was just such a big decision. One she didn't want to make on her own. She could discuss it with Daniel, but that would mean mixing her personal and professional lives. Even though she and Daniel had a good relationship, he was still her boss. She didn't want to give him the impression that she couldn't make a decision on her own. That wouldn't be doing her career any favors. Who wanted an indecisive lawyer?

What about Cade? She pushed the thought aside. She wasn't going to start making him more important in her life than she was in his. She'd traveled that road before and it was a dead end. She would have to decide whether or not to buy the house on her own. Fortunately she didn't need to make a decision right away. Her landlord had given her thirty days to decide. Surely she'd know which direction her life was taking her by then.

Chapter Eleven

"It's okay, sweet puppy," Megan called from across the barn, careful to keep her distance. Two days had passed since Cade had shown up at her house. Neither of them mentioned the conversation. It was as if they were both pretending it had never happened.

"Did you just call that dog sweet?" Cade asked, shaking his head. "No one would call that skunk-smelling animal sweet."

"I'm trying to make him feel better." She took a few cautious steps toward Tiny, who was whining pitifully.

"I'm not sure words are going to do it. That dog stinks."

"Shh." Megan stooped down in front of the dog and quickly covered his ears with her hands. This close, the dog smelled even worse, and she gagged and blinked back tears. She'd never smelled anything this bad in her life.

"He didn't understand a word I said," Cade protested. He filled two metal tubs with warm water.

"Still, he has feelings."

"He's slightly odoriferous. Is that better?"

She glared at him. "Not much."

"Fine. Would your puppy's delicate feelings be hurt if I said he is in desperate need of a bath?"

"I think those words would be acceptable."

"Good. So let's get to it."

"I only hope a bath helps." She didn't know how or when it happened, but Tiny and Gumball had dug a hole under the corral fence. Then, when no one was around, they'd squeezed under the fence and run off into the woods, where they'd had a run-in with a skunk. Apparently the encounter hadn't gone the dogs' way because they'd raced back to the corral with their tails tucked between their legs and reeking of skunk. They smelled so bad that the other dogs wouldn't let them come near. Poor shunned Tiny and Gumball had cowered and cried.

Megan lifted Tiny into a metal tub while Cade lifted Gumball, a slightly larger dog, into another one. The dogs struggled for a minute, fighting to get out of the water. Finally they relaxed and allowed Megan and Cade to smear on a homemade mixture of hydrogen peroxide, baking soda and dish washing liquid.

"Are you sure this is going to work?" To Megan's nose, the smell had gotten more intense, but that could be her imagination. She'd tried breathing through her mouth, but then she'd begun to taste the odor, which was infinitely worse. She'd rather hose off the dogs from a distance, but the soap had to be scrubbed in—and anyway, she knew that would only make Tiny and Gumball feel unwanted.

"It will. Trust me."

"I always thought tomato juice was the way to get rid of the smell." She looked at Cade as she rubbed the little dog's fur. A clump of suds dropped into the water and Tiny tried to eat it.

"That's one way. I've found that using this works best. We just work up a lather and then rinse it off. It might take more than one application before the skunk smell is entirely gone."

"And then you'll smell fresh as daisies," Megan said, including Tiny and Gumball in her promise. The dogs whined in response.

"Actually, they'll smell like wet dog."

"Well, wet dog will smell like daisies as far as I'm concerned."

Cade laughed and her stomach lurched a little. There was something about him that appealed to her as a woman. He was so sexy. But more than that, he made her heart happy. Being with him felt like home. And not in the physical sense, although she did enjoy being on the farm. There was something soothing about being outside in the open air. Relaxing on the glider in the shade of the trees had been the best. She'd do it every night if she could.

Being with Cade made her believe she could create a new family. Of course, that was before he'd decided that he didn't want a relationship with her. He'd run hot and cold the entire time she'd known him, as if uncertain about his feelings for her. Evidently he'd made up his mind and didn't want her. She didn't know what she'd done to make him feel that way, but there it was. And she'd tried to attach herself to other families enough times to know that it didn't work. She would have to content herself with being Cade's friend. Too bad her heart and body didn't seem to agree with that plan.

They washed and rinsed the dogs twice more before they took them out of the tubs and set them on the floor. Before Megan could grab a towel, Tiny took a step closer to her and shook out his fur. She squealed and held out her hands in front of her, but she ended up getting wet anyway. Cade laughed until Gumball shook out his fur as well, drenching him too.

Sitting down, Megan grabbed the towel and wiped off her face. She smirked. "Not so funny when it's you getting soaked, is it?"

Still laughing, Cade reached for her. She tried to scoot away but he was too quick for her. He sat down beside her then wrapped his arms around her waist. Immediately the room was filled with sexual tension and her heart began to beat faster. She looked into his eyes and the heat there had her freezing in place. Cade reached out slowly and brushed a lock of hair out of her face. His warm finger caressed her cheek and she shivered. Ever so slowly he lowered his head and gently kissed her lips.

At the contact, the blood began to race through her veins. The barn fell away and the barking dogs faded into the background. Suddenly Cade filled all of her senses. All she could see was Cade and the longing in his eyes. All she could feel was Cade and the heat emanating from his body, wrapping around hers. And in that moment, she didn't want more than Cade. She didn't need more than Cade.

Without thinking, she moved closer and draped her arms around his broad shoulders. When their lips met again, it was in an explosion of desire and fulfilled longing. The first kiss had been cautious and exploratory, as if Cade was unsure of her reaction. Since she was the one who'd initiated the second kiss, he didn't show any such restraint. This kiss was confident and hot and set every one of her nerve endings on fire. She was vaguely surprised that the heat from the kiss didn't turn the water on their clothes to steam.

She could have kissed him forever and might have tried if she hadn't felt a wet dog nose pressing against her side. Two wiggling furry bodies followed immediately as they tried to squeeze between her and Cade. She pulled back reluctantly and Tiny jumped onto her lap. Megan tried to meet Cade's gaze but he was busy struggling to get the other dog under control. She grabbed her towel and briskly rubbed the squirming body until the fur was almost dry.

"That's good enough," Cade said. "The sun will dry them the rest of the way. Let's put them back in the corral so I can fill that hole."

"Do you think they'll try to escape again?"

"Who knows? I didn't expect them to get out the first time. Maybe they learned their lesson with the skunk and they'll stay put. Or maybe they had so much fun on their adventure they'll try again. One thing is for sure. I'm not going to make it easy for them to get out next time."

They put Gumball and Tiny into the corral and the two dogs ran to join their friends. Now that they didn't stink to high heaven they were welcomed back into the fold.

"Need help filling the hole?"

"No. It's a one-man job."

"Okay." Megan's heart sank. Clearly the passionate kiss they'd shared didn't change anything between them. Or maybe it did. Maybe it clarified his feelings and Cade knew for certain that he didn't want her. Perhaps he'd felt the sexual tension that simmered below the surface and wanted to see if it fired up. But apparently it hadn't. At least not for him.

He grinned at her and tingles skittered down her spine. "I wouldn't mind company, though."

He grabbed a shovel with his right hand and then took her hand with his left. They walked side by side around the outside of the corral. When they reached the hole the dogs had used to get out of the corral, Cade shoveled the dirt back into the hole and patted it down firmly. He went to a nearby tree and scooped up another shovelful of dirt and pounded that in, as well. Just to be on the safe side, they circled the corral. Almost immediately they came upon another hole.

"Unbelievable," Megan said as Cade replaced the dirt.

"What is?"

"I thought they were happy here."

"I don't follow you. What does being happy have to do with digging holes? That's what dogs do."

"They had plenty of grass inside the corral if they only wanted to dig a hole. They were trying to run away."

"You're reading way too much into this. And I don't think they were trying to escape per se. I think they just wanted to see what was on the other side of the fence. And they did. But when they got into trouble, they raced back to the corral, a place where they knew they would be safe. They came back here because that's where you are. You're their safe place, Megan."

Megan smiled, and warmth bloomed in her heart at his words. She'd never been anyone's safe place. Truthfully, she'd never thought it was possible. After spending half of her life looking for a safe place to belong and not finding it yet, it had never occurred to her that she could provide that for someone else. It felt good even if that someone else was a dog. But in this instance, she didn't deserve the credit.

"It's not me. It's the corral and the other dogs."

"Why does it have to be one or the other? Can't it be both? The important thing is that the dogs feel safe here on the ranch. You gave them that."

"And you did, too."

"True." He reached back and patted himself on the shoulder. It was a silly thing for someone as serious as Cade to do. "I guess that makes me a hero."

"Okay, now you're getting a big head."

He laughed and they continued to walk around the corral. They found two more small holes, which Cade filled. Once they'd completed their circuit of the corral and filled all of the holes, they put away the shovel and returned to the corral to play with the dogs. They tossed the balls longer than usual, letting the dogs run off their excess energy. Megan set out bowls of fresh water and she and Cade left them to their own devices for a while.

"Hungry?" Cade asked.

Megan smiled. "Yes. And surprise, I brought lunch for you."

"Really?"

"Yes. I left it with your dad. He's keeping an eye on it for me."

"I'm intrigued. What are we having?"

"Nothing special. It's a slow-cooker beef and broccoli recipe I like. And before you ask, the beef and broccoli are certified organic. I just need to cook a pot of rice to go with it. And for dessert I made two different kinds of cookies. Chocolate chip and oatmeal raisin."

"And here I had you pegged as a turkey sandwich with a side salad for lunch person."

"When I'm working in the office that's true. There's a lot of work to do and a quick sandwich works best with my schedule. But on Saturdays I have a little more time to cook. Or I did before I took responsibility for Mrs. Crockett's pets."

They went inside Reginald's house. The smell of the cooking beef floated on the air and Megan's stomach growled. She didn't use the slow-cooker as much during the summer months as she did in the winter and fall. Maybe she would change that. Nothing was as enjoyable as being greeted by delicious aromas when she stepped into the house after a long day at work. It somehow transformed her rented house into something closer to a home.

Megan put rice and water into a pot and set it on the stove. "I started to bring the makings for a salad but then I remembered that I was coming to a farm. You have fresher vegetables than anything I could pick up at the store. Do you mind if I grab a few things from your garden?"

"My dad's garden is closer. He won't mind if you pick some vegetables. I'm sure he'll look at it as a fair trade for lunch. That is, if he's invited."

"Of course. That was never a question." Although she enjoyed spending time alone with Cade, she liked Reginald's company, too. Father and son might not live in the same house, but Megan knew they were a package deal and she was fine with that. In fact, she liked it.

She took the basket Cade offered and went back outside. The garden was enormous and she squealed in delight. It contained every type of vegetable she'd need for a salad as well as those that would make tasty side dishes. After filling her basket, she returned to the kitchen. Cade had set the table and she was surprised that there were only two plates.

"Your dad's not willing to eat my food?" She was only half joking. Reginald had cooked for her many times and she'd been looking forward to returning the favor.

"Nothing like that. One of Dad's friends just invited him to town for an early dinner and then they're going bowling. Mom and Dad used to belong to a bowling league. They were really good and won several trophies over the years. When Mom got sick they dropped out. Dad hasn't picked up his ball since."

"It sounds like your parents were an especially close couple."

Cade grinned. "They met in grammar school, if you can believe it. Dad always said he didn't like Mom but that she had a crush on him. Mom swore it was the other way around. When they were in high school, their best friends started dating. Mom's best friend was only allowed to go out in a group or on double dates, so Mom and Dad were thrown together a lot. It was rough going for a while. They were either bickering or ignoring each other."

Megan rinsed the vegetables and began cutting them into two bowls. "And then your mom and dad fell in love?"

"Not right away. Whenever they went to the movies, rather than sit with their friends, Mom and Dad sat as far away from each other as they could and still be in the same theater. Same with dinner. Their friends would eat together and Mom and Dad would get separate tables on opposite sides of the restaurant."

"That's…uh."

"Insane?"

Megan laughed. "I was going to say extreme, but insane works, too."

"One night they were at the movies when this other guy starts to talk to my mom. I don't think she liked him. Anyway, my dad stepped up and said she was his date and to leave her alone. Mom didn't disagree. Instead she ordered a huge bucket of popcorn, a large pop and about five different kinds of candy and left it up to Dad to pay for them. She was his date after all."

"And then it was love?" Megan surmised as she put the salads on the table. The rice had cooked, and she spooned it onto two plates and then added the beef and broccoli.

"It took a while. They were both stubborn and neither one wanted to be the first to admit they liked the other. But they did start sitting together at the movies and whenever they went to eat. Eventually they started dating. Then they fell in love and got married."

"And are their friends still together?"

"No. They broke up a couple of months after Mom and Dad got together. They were the maid of honor and best man at the wedding a few years later, and from what I was told, they barely managed to be civil to each other."

Megan laughed. "Well, I guess their job was just to get your parents together."

"That's what Mom always said."

Cade warmed up some rolls his father had made for dinner the previous night and set them on the table.

"What was your mom like?" Megan asked as they started to eat.

Cade took a sip of ice water before answering. "She was great. No one who met her ever forgot her. She had a magnetic personality and lit up the room the second she walked in. When she and my dad were together you could see the love between them. I could actually feel it. When she died, I didn't think my dad would survive. He withdrew into himself and shut the world out. He would sit in his chair for days on end and just stare at the wall. It was as if part of him had climbed into her grave with her. It's taken a while, but he's becoming more of his old self."

"Losing her must have left a hole in your life, too."

Cade nodded. "Yes. It was so hard watching her die, but I selfishly didn't want to let her go. I could tell she was hurting, but I knew once she was gone it would be forever. I wouldn't see her again. Wouldn't be able to tell her how much I loved her. I didn't want that day to ever come. Sometimes I wonder if it would have been better not knowing she was going to die."

"No."

"I'm sorry, Megan. That was insensitive."

"You said what you felt. There's nothing wrong with that. I just wish I had known I was going to lose everyone I loved. I could have told them goodbye and how much I loved them. How much I always would."

"They knew, Megan." His soft voice comforted her. "They knew."

She blinked back tears, then forced a smile. This was supposed to be a happy time. Earlier Cade had kissed her in a way that had all but had her wanting to break into song. Of course, since she couldn't carry a tune in a basket, it was best that she'd refrained. Even now, the kiss was still on her mind. "Are we going to talk about what happened in the barn earlier?"

"You mean when you tackled and kissed me?"

Megan sputtered and set her fork on her plate. "That's

not the way I would describe it, but yes, I would like to talk about the kiss. What does it mean and where do we go from here?"

He set down his fork as well and gave her his full attention. "I don't know, Megan. It was a simple kiss."

"Okay." It wasn't what she wanted to hear, but she appreciated his honesty. "I wasn't expecting a marriage proposal. I just don't want things to become weird between us again."

"I know. I guess I deserve that." He leaned back in his chair and looked at her. "You don't know much about me, do you?"

"If you mean gossipy stuff, no. The only thing I know about you is what you've told me."

"Yeah. You don't strike me as the type to talk about people behind their backs."

"I'm not." She'd been the subject of gossip for half of her life. Some of the conversations had been well-meaning, but a lot had been downright cruel. She made it a practice not to talk about a person who wasn't present and able to make sure what was being said was the absolute truth.

"Up until a few months ago I was engaged," Cade said.

"You were? What happened?"

"She decided she didn't want to get married—at least not to me—and she ended it."

Megan's head spun. Cade had been engaged. And he hadn't been the one to break it off. Was he still in love with her? Did he hope with time to win her back? Megan had been falling for him and imagining a future together, and Cade had doubtless been longing for the woman he'd wanted to marry. No wonder he'd been so grumpy when they met. He'd been trying to make it through the day with a broken heart.

"Wow. Do you run into her a lot?" One of the benefits of moving from New York had been knowing she'd never see Tim again.

"No. She moved to Chicago shortly thereafter."

That was a relief. Megan wasn't sure what was going on between her and Cade, but she didn't relish the idea of encountering the woman he'd wanted to marry. On the other hand, it would be nice to see what kind of woman Cade found attractive. He was the definition of a rugged man who spent all of his time outdoors, so no doubt his fiancée shared that in common with him. She probably grew up on the neighboring farm and planned to work beside him on a daily basis. Maybe Cade and his fiancée had been like his parents and had been in love since high school. One thing was for sure, she was probably nothing like Megan. If that wasn't proof that he could never be attracted to her, then she didn't know what was.

Chapter Twelve

"I talked to Rebekah today. They have space for two more dogs," Megan said the next day.

"That's good." Cade closed the last barn door, then led Samson and Delilah to his truck. The other cats and dogs were settled for the night. He couldn't believe how quickly the day had sped by. He'd enjoyed every second he'd spent in Megan's company. Although the weekend was coming to an end, it wasn't quite over. They still had Sunday dinner ahead of them. Two steaks were marinating in his special sauce. He'd throw them on the grill as soon as they got back to his house. "You wanted to find good homes for them, remember?"

"I know. It was easier in the beginning, but I've gotten attached to them. I don't want to say goodbye to any more of them."

"But you always knew this was temporary. A stop-gap until they could find their forever homes. And it sounds like they're one step closer."

"My rational mind knows this, but my heart isn't ready to let them go."

He understood. He'd grown attached to Delilah and couldn't imagine not having her there every night. And of course Delilah was so close to Samson. Cade had to admit the cat had grown on him. He hoped that they managed to find a home together. It didn't seem right to separate them. "Do you know which ones you'll take?"

"I was thinking about Tiny and Gumball. They are so rambunctious and playful. I can picture a family with kids being happy with either of them. Of course, they might also be good company for an older person living alone. I just want them to end up in good, loving homes. I want them to find good families."

She worried about the animals the same way a mother worried about her kids, wanting only the best for them. Even though she was struggling with the thought of separating, he knew she wanted them to find a forever home.

"They'll be well cared for. I've known Birdie and Bunny for years. They wouldn't allow just anyone to adopt from the rescue. And you're the one who told me that Rebekah checks out all of the families as part of the process. They'll be going to good homes. And this time they won't have to leave."

Megan smiled, but he could tell her heart wasn't in it. There were no words that could erase her anxiety. She'd worry about the animals until she felt comfortable with their situation, and nothing he said would change that. He wrapped his arm around her shoulder, and what he'd intended to be a quick and comforting hug rapidly morphed into something different the second he touched her warm skin. Her sweet scent teased him and he was filled with desire. He wanted to kiss her again like he had yesterday, but he resisted the urge. They were getting too close too fast. Sure he could envision them together, but he could just as easily picture her walking away from him. And until he was sure one way or the other, he was going to protect his heart the best way he knew how.

A smarter man would have kept her at a distance, but no one had ever accused his of being all that smart. Besides, how was he supposed to determine if she had what it took to stick around if he was never around her? And truthfully, the more time they spent together, the more he was convinced that she intended to make Spring Forest her permanent home.

He held her for a long moment, then gently set her away from him and helped her into the truck. They drove to his house in companionable silence. He got the fire going in the grill, then helped Megan prepare the side dishes. They'd spent time together the past week and had joint meal preparation down to a science. Once the flames had died down, he put the steaks on the rack. The sizzle preceded the aroma by a few seconds and his stomach rumbled. While the steaks cooked, he took a seat at the patio table. Megan lit the candles on the table and then sat down beside him.

"How is your business coming?" Megan asked.

"Good. I got two more email inquiries in response to some advertising."

"Really? That's great. Are you going to be able to get them what they need?"

He nodded with satisfaction. "Yep. One is a catering company that specializes in corporate events, and the other is a new restaurant with twelve tables. Each business is small enough that I can handle everything on my own for the time being. I think I have a good system in place, but working with small, local businesses like these will help me work out all of the bugs. I want to make sure that I haven't missed anything important before I start adding more clients."

Megan jumped up and squeezed him around the neck, then kissed his cheek. "I'm so happy for you. Once people get a taste of your food, they'll be lining up around the block to buy it."

"You're a bit biased, but I hope you're right."

"Of course I'm right. I'm a woman."

He laughed, then told her more about his potential clients before checking the steaks. "Two more minutes ought to do it."

"Okay." She went inside and brought out the salads and a pitcher of lemonade and set them on the table. Although he drank the occasional beer, he wasn't much of a drinker. Megan didn't drink alcoholic beverages at all. But then, given the way her family had been killed, he wasn't surprised. In her situation, he wouldn't drink intoxicating beverages either.

The steaks were done so he put them on the plates beside the pasta salad. Once they'd begun to eat, he looked up at her. "Anything new and exciting going on in your life?"

She frowned. "Well, it's not necessarily new or exciting, but my landlord is selling the house that he's renting to me."

"Wow. When?"

"He's going to put it on the market in about three weeks."

"That doesn't give you much time to find something else."

"No. But he has offered to sell it to me if I'm interested in it."

"So, what are you going to do? Are you thinking about buying it?"

"I'm not sure. I like the house, but it seems like a big commitment. And it's so permanent. I've made so many changes in my life recently. I'm still trying to get my bearings. I'm not sure if buying the house would be the right thing to do right now. On the other hand, if I don't, I'll have to find another place to live. That'll be a hassle." She sighed. "I'm not sure what's right for me."

As he listened, his hopes sank. She thought buying the house would be too permanent? Did that mean she wanted to be able to pick up and move again? If not, then why was she struggling to decide? To his way of thinking, it was an easy decision. If she really wanted to commit to living in Spring Forest, she'd buy the house. She'd told him that she liked it and that it felt welcoming. True, buying a house was a big deal, but it made more sense than renting for years.

One thing was clear to him—she wanted to keep her

options open—including the choice to leave the town and him behind.

"What do you think I should do?"

Buy the house and stay with me.

"I can't make that decision for you." He'd tried to convince Deadra to stay and she'd ignored his pleas. For all her talk of being in love with him and wanting to spend her life by his side, she'd forgotten about him fast enough. She'd barely taken off his ring before she'd put on one from another man. Then she'd jumped on the first jet to Chicago and hadn't looked back. Not that he was waiting to hear from her. When he was done with a relationship, he put the woman in the past. Deadra was securely in his past. But the lessons she'd taught him wouldn't be fading anytime soon.

"I don't expect you to make the decision for me. But we're friends. And friends discuss things and give their opinions. I promise I won't blame you if it doesn't work out. I just want to know what you think."

"Okay. I think you should buy the house."

She nodded. Her expression didn't change so he didn't know whether he'd given her the answer she'd wanted. But he'd given her an honest answer.

"Okay. Why? I'll probably put a pro and con list together, so I need all the arguments we can think of."

"That makes sense. Right off the top of my head I can think of several reasons. It's a nice house and you seem happy there. It's close to your job. And you won't have to try and find another place to live, which you described as a hassle."

"Those are valid points. Thank you."

She picked up her knife and fork and began to tackle her dinner once more. "This has got to be the best steak that I've eaten in my life. Maybe you should think about handling both ends of the farm-to-table business and open your own restaurant."

"I don't think my new client would appreciate the competition."

"Probably not."

He wanted to talk more about her thought process as it related to buying the house, but he didn't want to press her. Besides, he wasn't sure how he would react if she said that she was leaning toward not buying the house. He knew he might be reading more into this decision than he should. Not buying the house didn't mean she had one foot out the door. It might mean she wasn't looking to buy real estate right now. He needed to calm down. He had to stop comparing her to Deadra, who had never been happy in Spring Forest.

Megan managed to keep the conversation light as she finished her dinner and dessert even as Cade's words echoed in her mind. He wanted her to buy the house, thereby making a long-term commitment to live somewhere else. She'd thought they were growing closer. By necessity they'd spent time together while they took care of the cats and dogs. But they'd also begun to confide in each other. She'd told him things she hadn't shared with anyone else, baring her soul. And he'd done the same. She'd begun to imagine them falling in love and maybe eventually getting married. Then she would move into his house on the farm, where they would live happily-ever-after. She'd have a family again.

Once more she'd let her imagination get the best of her. They weren't going to be together on his farm or anywhere else. Not if he wanted her to live in town.

How many times was she going to be rejected before she learned her lesson? Each of her foster families had used her and then turned her away. And then Tim and his family had done the same. Oh, they hadn't used her, but they'd kicked her out of the family and forgotten she'd ever existed. Each time she'd thought she'd found a family again, reality slapped her in the face. She wasn't wanted.

Maybe it was time to let that dream go once and for all and be satisfied with what she had. And she had a lot.

She had good friends who she could count on in a pinch. Friends who liked being around her and who made her laugh. Not everyone could say that. Though she'd wanted him to be more, she could still count Cade as a friend. Maybe it was time to do that and stop expecting more from him.

"Dinner was delicious. I know you have to get up early and so do I. If you don't mind, I'll stop by before I go to work in the morning and pick up the dogs. That way I can get them to the shelter as soon as it opens. If I wait to come out here until after work, it'll be too late."

"Why don't I bring them around lunchtime? That way it'll save you a trip."

"Can you call me when you get there so I can meet you?"

"Don't you trust me?" He winked so she knew he was joking.

"Of course. I just want to tell them goodbye." And she wanted to let them know that they would be okay in the shelter, and that it would lead to them finding wonderful new homes. She hadn't had anyone to reassure her of that when she'd been moved from house to house. After a while she'd taken to reassuring herself as she stood on a strange doorstep, all her earthly goods in a bag at her feet. Those carefully chosen words of comfort hadn't always been true for her, but maybe the dogs will be luckier.

"I'll call you when I get there."

He didn't say as much as he dropped her at her car. As she drove away, she thought about how he'd wanted her to buy the house, and she couldn't help wondering if she would ever be loved.

That thought haunted her dreams, and for the first time since she'd moved to Spring Forest, she was plagued by nightmares. After tossing and turning most of the night, she rose with the sun and went to work early. Working was preferable to dwelling on the fact that Cade was never going to love her.

She took a quick shower, toasted a bagel and brewed green tea, which she poured into her I Heart New York travel mug. The drive to the office was quick. As expected, the lights were off when she arrived, but that wasn't a problem. Daniel had given her a key soon after she'd started to work for him. Juggling her briefcase and mug, she unlocked the door and turned on the light in the reception area before entering her office. While waiting for her computer to boot, she scanned her calendar for the week. When her eyes hit Saturday, she saw that she'd scribbled a note about a black tie fundraiser that would be held in Raleigh. The tickets were a gift from a client and she'd been waffling about whether or not to attend. At the time she'd been given the tickets, she'd been new to town and hadn't known a soul. Now she wondered if Cade would go with her if she asked.

She could absolutely picture Cade dressed in a tuxedo. With his broad shoulders, muscular chest and narrow waist, he would easily be the best-looking man there. That is, if he went with her. But first she had to invite him. Would she? That was the question. Of course she would. They were friends. She'd ask him this afternoon when the met at the shelter. But wondering whether or not he would agree to accompany her tied her stomach in knots.

She forced that worry aside and got to work. She was busy finalizing the paperwork for the Whitaker sisters to give to the prosecutor so he could file charges against their brother when Emma stuck her head in.

"Hey, you're here awfully early."

Megan smiled and waved at her friend to come on in. "I was up early and didn't see a need to putter around the house when there was work to be done. Besides, I need to run by the pet shelter around noon to drop off a couple of dogs. I'm not sure how long that'll take, so I figured I'd get as much work done now as I could."

"How many animals have gone to the shelter so far?"

"These two make nine out of sixteen. That only leaves seven on Cade's farm."

Emma raised her eyebrows. "Cade, is it? Sounds like the two of you are getting closer."

Megan laughed. "Maybe."

"So you no longer think he's the grumpiest man in Spring Forest."

Megan had forgotten she'd said that. "No. I just needed to get to know him better. And he needed to get to know me."

After looking at her watch, Emma stood. "Good. I need to get to work. I'll see you later."

Megan's morning went smoothly, but she jumped in anticipation each time her phone rang. Silly as it was, she watched the clock as she waited for Cade to call. She had it bad and as the old saying went, that wasn't good. Despite her nerves, she did manage to have three intelligent business conversations, one with another attorney and two with clients.

Promptly at noon her phone rang. Her voice was breathless as she said hello and she pinched herself, hoping the pain would chase away the nerves.

"Hi. I'm on my way to the shelter. I should be there in a few minutes. Don't rush, I'll wait for you to get there." Unlike hers, Cade's voice was strong and steady.

"I'm leaving now."

"See you then. Bye."

"Bye." She hung up the phone. She'd hoped for something more personal. He hadn't even asked how her day was going. Still, it was ridiculous to be disappointed. They didn't need to have a long conversation now. They'd see each other in under half an hour.

Megan grabbed the paperwork she needed to drop off to the Whitaker sisters and tossed it into her briefcase. She'd talked to them this morning to let them know she would be bringing by the documents today. Megan had kept her promise and hadn't put pressure on Birdie or Bunny. In fact, she hadn't mentioned it again. Perhaps Doc J had talked to them about it. He had been really concerned about their welfare. Whatever the catalyst, Megan was glad they'd reached this decision. No one should get away with taking advantage of these two sweet women. Birdie and Bunny protected animals and helped them find their forever homes. The sisters deserved to be protected as well.

She waved to Emma and headed for the shelter. As she got nearer, butterflies began fluttering in her stomach. This was getting ridiculous. Cade wasn't the first man she'd ever been attracted to. Tim had been good-looking and she'd found him quite appealing. Yet despite the fact that he'd been her fiancé, she'd never reacted to him this way. She was positively giddy in anticipation of seeing Cade again.

And it was more than the physical attraction she felt for Cade. It was everything about him. It was the way he took care of his father and included Reginald in his life. It was the way he cared for Mrs. Crockett's animals when he was under no obligation to do so. It was the way he listened to her and held her in his arms after she'd broken down. Cade's kindness was even more attractive than his gorgeous body, which was saying something. Was it any wonder she was falling in love with him?

She inhaled deeply as the thought reverberated in her mind. Did she just think that she was falling in love with Cade Battle? It was okay if she liked and admired him. She didn't even mind if she had a crush on him. But she didn't like thinking she was in love with him. Not when he wasn't thinking along the same lines.

Sure, he'd kissed her a couple of times. If she was fifteen or sixteen she might make the mistake of thinking that meant he felt something special for her. But she was twenty-eight and knew better than to read more into a few kisses than was intended. A kiss wasn't a commitment to her. That he wanted her to buy a house was proof that he wasn't trying to establish a long-term relationship with her. If he'd been interested in her he wouldn't want her to settle into a home somewhere else. He'd want her with him. Which was why she couldn't start thinking about falling in love with him. They were friends, just friends.

Despite her lecture to keep her cool, Megan touched up her lipstick and brushed her hair before she got out of the car. Cade wasn't there yet, so she went inside the shelter. After talking with the volunteer at the desk, she went to the back where the animals were being housed. They all looked happy and well cared for. They were clean and appeared healthy. She knew Tiny and Gumball would be safe and loved while they waited for their new families to find them. She couldn't ask for more.

"Hey."

Megan jumped and turned at the sound of Cade's voice. He was dressed in his customary jeans and long-sleeved shirt. Even though she'd been expecting him, her heart began to pound in her chest. "Hi."

Tiny and Gumball were on leashes beside him, and she knelt down and gave each dog a hug. She felt her eyes well with tears. She tried to blink them back but a couple of them fell. This wasn't going to be easy.

"Hey, they're going to be fine. They're going to find their forever homes and be loved for the rest of their lives."

She sniffed. "I know that. I was just telling myself the same thing. That's why I don't understand why I'm reacting this way."

"No? I do." He wiped a tear from her cheek. "It's because you love them."

"I do. And I'm going to miss them."

"So will I. Which is why it's important that we all get the opportunity to say goodbye."

"Thanks for being here."

"Of course."

The dogs began licking her face. Laughter bubbled up inside her and she sat on the floor, not caring if her black suit pants got dirty. Never in her life would she have imagined such a scene. Tiny climbed on her lap and she rubbed him, then gave him a big hug. Not to be outdone, Gumball nudged her elbow until she lifted her arm and let him join in the group hug.

Megan held them for a while, rubbing their soft fur and scratching behind their ears. "I'm going to miss you guys so much."

They barked in reply, then jumped off her lap. Apparently their goodbyes had been said and they were ready to start the next adventure in their lives. Cade gave them a last rub and then helped Megan to her feet. Instead of letting go of her hand as she had expected, he held on and gave it a gentle squeeze. A teenage volunteer had joined them while they were saying goodbye, and he stood by silently. Cade handed the kid the leashes, and Megan watched as the teen led the dogs to the back of the shelter where they'd live until their new families found them.

"Do you want to go with them?" Cade asked.

"No. I don't think I can bear to say goodbye again. Besides, I don't want to confuse them. If we go with them, they might expect to go back home with us. And I think they've already said their goodbyes."

"Then let's get out of here."

She let Cade lead her out of the shelter and into the parking lot. If she could plan her day over again, she wouldn't have scheduled her meeting with Birdie and Bunny for right now. But at the time it had seemed like a good idea. She hadn't imagined becoming an emotional basket case from saying goodbye to the dogs. Once she and Cade were alone outside, he wrapped her in his arms and held her. The feel of his hands as he rubbed her back was at once soothing and arousing. After a few minutes the sorrow in her heart had been replaced by longing and she lifted her head. His eyes met hers and he lowered his head and brushed his lips across hers.

Aware that they were in a public place, Megan forced down the desire to deepen the kiss and stepped back. Her lips were tingling too much for her to try and form words.

Cade rubbed a hand over his closely cropped hair as if he needed a moment to get his feelings under control, as well. Seeing him so affected emboldened her and before she could give in to her doubts, she blurted out her question. "Do you want to go out with me this Saturday?"

He blinked, and Megan wished she could call back

the words and pretend that she hadn't asked him. Then he smiled. "I'd love to. Where are we going?"

"To a fundraiser in Raleigh."

"What kind of fundraiser?"

"A black tie dinner. One of my clients bought the tickets, but since she's unable to go, she gave them to me. There's going to be dancing and a silent auction also. It's all to raise money for school supplies for needy kids as well as to fund several college scholarships."

After a long moment he nodded. "It sounds like a worthy cause. And it might be fun."

"So you're saying that you'll go with me?" She barely managed to keep the surprise from her voice.

"Why not. I like to dance."

"Great. I'll call you later with the details."

Cade smiled and then climbed into the truck. She watched as he drove away before she headed over to the Whitaker sisters' house. Birdie was outside, and she greeted Megan warmly when she arrived. "Come on inside. We'll have tea and sandwiches before we get started."

Megan smiled. "I'd appreciate it."

They walked through the old house and into the kitchen. Bunny was placing a platter of sandwiches on the table, and she smiled at Megan. "Have a seat."

"Thank you." Megan knew that the sisters didn't like to discuss business while they ate, so she didn't bring up their brother or what he'd done. They asked her about the dogs she'd brought into the shelter, and once more her eyes welled with tears. She didn't know why she kept getting emotional. They were only dogs and not even her own. But still her heart was breaking at the thought of never seeing them again. She told herself that they would be happy with their new families, but that didn't ease the pain in her heart.

"Animals have a way of stealing your heart," Birdie said, patting Megan's hand.

"They sure do," Megan agreed.

"We've fallen in love with a lot of the animals that have come our way over the years," Bunny added. "Some of them we've kept, but others we've had to let go."

"How do you manage that?" Megan asked softly.

"By acknowledging that Birdie and I aren't the only people with love in our hearts for animals. We aren't the only two people in the world who can give them good homes. Since we know that, we trust that they'll be just as happy somewhere else."

"That makes sense," Megan said. She was coming to see that there were a lot of loving people in the world. Especially out in North Carolina.

"It doesn't make the pain in our hearts any less," Bunny warned. "It just doesn't last as long."

"That's something," Megan said. "Thank you."

The sisters nodded and they resumed eating. Megan's heart was lighter and she was grateful for the sisters' understanding.

Once they had finished eating, Megan handed the sisters the papers they needed in order to press charges against their brother. She spoke gently because she knew it couldn't be easy to take this step. True, he'd hurt them, but they still loved him. She knew that if her brother had betrayed her like this, she'd still love him. But then, Marlon had been a good guy. He'd been her hero. He'd never have done anything this devious to her or anyone else.

"We've talked to the sheriff and the prosecutor." Birdie sounded sad, and Megan's heart ached for her. Still, Megan knew she was doing the right thing. If they hadn't stopped their brother, they would have ended up destitute. They might even have lost their home just like Mrs. Crockett had. Who knew what would have happened then?

Megan took each sister by the hand, then gave a reassuring squeeze. "You're doing the right thing."

"We know," Bunny said. "It just hurts a little bit right now. It'll stop."

Megan knew the sisters needed to be alone to mourn, so she closed her briefcase and stood. When Birdie looked like she was going to stand too, Megan stopped her. "Don't get up. I know my way out. Feel free to call me anytime if either of you needs me."

"Thanks, Megan," Bunny said and then linked hands with Birdie.

Megan nodded and then left, but the image of the sisters holding on to each other for support stayed with her as she drove back to the office. They might be hurting now, but at least they had each other to turn to for comfort. That had to help.

Chapter Thirteen

Megan looked critically at her reflection in the mirror. She turned slightly in order to get a good view of her profile, then shimmied a little to see what she would look like when she danced. Pretty good if she did say so herself. The dress didn't pull or stretch when she moved. Nor did it gap away from her breasts. Best of all, she looked good in it.

She blew out a breath. Finally. It had taken six tries but she'd finally found a winner. The silver dress fit as if it had been made specifically for her. And to top it off, she'd found the perfect shoes in the exact same shade with the right height heels. It was as if her fairy godmother had put everything together and then placed the various items around the store. Of course, a fairy godmother would have been cheaper. Neither the dress nor the shoes had been on sale.

Ordinarily Megan wouldn't spend this much money on a dress she knew she wouldn't wear more than a couple of times. She didn't live the kind of lifestyle that required formal dresses. Even when she'd lived in New York, her entertainment had been limited to dinner and movies with friends, with the occasional Broadway show thrown in just to switch things up. And she'd been fine with that. Megan didn't have anything against fancy parties, especially if they were for a good cause, which this one was. She just preferred quiet evenings at home reading a book or with a small gathering of friends.

But this wasn't going to be just any old formal dinner with any old date. She was going out with Cade Battle and needed to look her absolute best. And in this dress she definitely would.

After taking one last look at herself, she slipped off the dress and put her suit back on. Although Daniel was a good boss who didn't monitor her every move, Megan had come in early and worked through lunch the past three days because she knew she was going to go shopping in Raleigh today and didn't want to rush. She grabbed the hangers holding the rejected dresses in one hand and the chosen one in the other. After hanging the unwanted dresses on the rack outside the dressing room, Megan purchased her dress and shoes.

She had the perfect earrings and necklace at home to complete the look. She could hardly wait for tomorrow to arrive. Of course, she needed to get past today first. There had been room for two more cats at the shelter and Cade had dropped them off today. Even though Megan had already planned to go shopping today, she knew she wouldn't have gone with Cade to drop off the cats. It was just too hard to say a final goodbye to them. Knowing they were going to find good homes didn't take away the heartbreak she felt when she thought about never seeing them again. There'd been too many final goodbyes in her lifetime to subject herself to more. She knew Cade would reassure them that they would be okay.

She stopped at home and raced inside to hang up her dress and drop her new shoes on the floor before heading back to the office. The afternoon flew, and before she knew it she was on her way out to the farm. The number of animals had diminished so greatly that cleaning up after them was a breeze. She tossed the ball to the dogs and then rubbed the cats that were in the mood for attention. As usual, Samson was near Delilah, but he allowed her to carry him around.

"You're my favorite," she said, rubbing her nose into his fur. "But that will be our secret."

"What secret is that?"

Megan spun around to face Cade. He was grinning at her as if he'd caught her with her hand in the cookie jar. No matter how many times she saw him, being near him made her heart skip a beat. And when he smiled at her like he was doing now, it took all of her self-control not to fling herself at him and plead with him to love her. But of course she wouldn't. When Tim had broken up with her, she'd all but begged him not to leave her. It hadn't mattered that she knew he was right to face the truth that their relationship wasn't working anymore. She just hadn't wanted to be alone.

She wasn't going to do that again. Cade had made

it clear that he wasn't interested in pursuing a relationship. Since his engagement had ended much as hers had, she understood his reluctance. And if he was still in love with the other woman, that could only mean heartache for Megan. She'd had more than enough of that. It was better for her well-being that they merely remained friends. Not every two people were destined to be together. Just because being around him made her float on air didn't mean he had to feel the same.

"So, I take it you're not going to tell me your secret?"

"Nope."

His eyes shifted to Samson, who purred, and back to Megan's. "That's okay. I think I can guess."

"Yes, you probably can." At least *that* secret. She'd never let him know how much she liked him.

"What were you doing?" she asked, pointing to the shovel he was carrying.

"Ever since Gumball and Tiny escaped, I've been checking the fence surrounding the corral regularly to make sure none of the other dogs decide to make a break for it."

"Find any holes?"

"Not a one. I guess they were the only ones looking for adventure. Or maybe coming back smelling like skunk scared the others off the idea."

She placed Samson on the rail and watched as the cat crossed the fence until he was near Delilah. Once there, Samson sat down and began to lick his paws.

"Do you think the other animals wonder where they've gone?"

"Tiny and Gumball?"

"All of them. It's like they're here one day and gone the next. Do you think they notice?"

"Of course they notice. They lived together for a long time. Do they worry about them and miss them? I have no idea."

"Do you think they'll forget their time together on the farm? Will they forget us?"

"Again, I don't know for certain if they'll remember being here. But I think they'll always remember you and the love you gave them."

She crossed the yard and gave him a big hug. Somehow he'd known just what she needed to hear. She started to pull back, but he pulled her closer, holding her in his arms a while longer. Pressed against his muscular chest, she inhaled and got a lungful of his scent, and her eyes closed. There was something so familiar and comforting about Cade. Something about being in his arms felt like home even as she was turned on.

A cat wound around their legs, interrupting the embrace. Megan reluctantly stepped out of Cade's arms and picked up Molly. "I guess she's trying to let me know that they're ready to eat."

"Yeah." Cade didn't seem too happy about the interruption, which made Megan smile. Maybe he enjoyed holding her in his arms as much as she enjoyed being there.

After they'd taken care of the animals, Cade walked her to her car. She had a nail appointment she didn't want to miss. "I'll take care of feeding them in the morning. Dad said he'll take care of them tomorrow night while we're out so we don't have to worry about that."

"Thanks. You and your dad are the best."

"I'll pick you up at six. See you tomorrow." He brushed his lips across hers and then opened her car door to let her inside.

Her lips tingled all the way home.

Cade loosened the tie and started again. He hated black tie events. Hated wearing a tuxedo. He blew out a breath and leaned against his dresser. Maybe *hate* was too harsh a word. He wasn't vehemently opposed to formal functions, especially those designed to raise money for good causes. He just didn't enjoy attending them. He'd rather donate the cost of the ticket and stay home and watch a game on television. Deadra had loved rubbing elbows with the movers and shakers of the world and had dragged him to more than enough charity balls and high-priced dinners to last a lifetime. He'd hoped those days were behind him and that he'd never have to wear a tuxedo again. Yet here he was, struggling with a bow tie so he could escort another big-city woman to yet another fancy shindig.

He'd tried not to compare Megan and Deadra, but they had so many similarities it would be foolish to ignore them. They both moved from big cities for new jobs and claimed to want to live a quiet life in Spring Forest. Deadra had lasted long enough for him to fall in love and propose. Theirs had been a whirlwind affair that he'd believed would lead to a lifetime of happiness. He'd been wrong about that.

His relationship with Megan was traveling on pretty

much the same path, and Cade couldn't help but wonder if he was making another mistake.

So why hadn't he told Megan no when she asked him to go with her? Because he was a fool who couldn't get enough of being around her. It was as if she'd put a spell on him, leaving him powerless to resist her. He wanted to believe that she was different from Deadra and that she'd actually stick it out in Spring Forest. He wouldn't make the mistake of engaging in a whirlwind affair this time. No, he'd take his time and get to know her. He'd date her for months instead of mere weeks. He just needed a sign that she planned to put down roots in Spring Forest before he put his heart on the line. Maybe if they dated a while, her true intentions would become clear.

That decided, he pulled on the tie, and this time he knotted it perfectly. After checking the time, he loaded Samson and Delilah into his truck and drove to his dad's house. When they arrived he put them into the corral. Reginald was leaning against the fence. When he saw Cade he let out a long whistle.

"Don't you look spiffy," his dad said, straightening and coming closer. "Let's go inside before you get all dusty. I want to get a picture."

Cade managed not to roll his eyes at his father's enthusiasm. It wasn't as if he was going to prom. But since his father was in such good spirits, Cade wouldn't rain on his parade. It had been so painful watching his father suffer as he mourned the loss of Cade's mother. Thankfully he'd gradually become his old self again.

If Cade had to put a date on it, the change began

about the time the animals came to the farm. But Cade knew the animals didn't deserve credit for the happiness that had been floating in the air on Battle Lands Farm these past weeks. That honor belonged to Megan. She'd brought so much life and joy with her each day that it had become part of the atmosphere.

"Hold still," Reginald said, aiming his phone's camera at Cade. "Okay, now smile."

Cade smiled and at Reginald's direction struck a couple of poses. After a few minutes, Reginald set down the phone.

"Done?"

"Yes." Reginald sighed. "I just wish I could have a picture of you and Megan together."

"That won't be a problem. These places generally have a photographer. I'll make sure we pose for a couple of pictures and give you a copy."

"Thanks." Reginald reached in his pocket and pulled out his car keys. "I cleaned and waxed it. I even put in one of those fancy scented things. It should smell like baby powder."

"You didn't need to go to all that trouble."

"You can't expect Megan to get into a dirty car dressed in her fancy clothes."

Which was why Cade was borrowing his father's car. He didn't want Megan trying to climb into his truck wearing a long dress. "You're right. Thank you."

"It was my pleasure. I like Megan. She's a special girl. In a way she reminds me of your mother. She's the kind of girl you can count on when things get rough. The kind of girl you marry."

Cade sighed. His dad would go on for hours about Megan's virtues. But Cade didn't have hours. Megan was waiting for him. He held up the keys and headed for the door. "Thanks again. See you tonight."

As he drove to Megan's house, Cade thought about his father's praise. His father was a good judge of character. He could tell the real thing from a fake from miles away. And it didn't take him long to see a person's true nature. Not only that, Reginald wasn't given to false or overblown flattery. If he thought Megan was the real deal, that carried a lot of weight with Cade. It was a good thing that Reginald liked Megan since no matter how hard he fought against it, Cade was becoming emotionally involved with her. He decided not to fight his feelings tonight. Instead he'd simply enjoy himself and let the evening flow.

The drive was quick, and before he knew it he was standing on Megan's front porch. He rang the doorbell, then fussed with his tie to make sure it was straight. The door swung open and there she was. He took one look at her and nearly gasped. He'd known she was beautiful, but he'd never seen her looking like this. Dressed in a silk silver dress that clung to her spectacular curves, she was absolutely stunning. Her subtle makeup accentuated her high cheekbones, lush lips and bright eyes.

Clearly unaware of how deeply affected he was, she stepped back and let him into her house. "I just need to grab my purse and the tickets."

Not trusting his voice to come out in anything other than an adolescent boy's squeak, he nodded and then swallowed. He gave himself a mental shake and ordered himself to snap out of his stupor. It wasn't as if he hadn't seen a pretty woman wearing a sexy dress before. He had, plenty of times. But none of them had looked this good. Not that Megan's dress was overly sexy. It was pretty tame compared to some of what he'd seen other women wearing. But looking at them hadn't made his knees turn to Jell-O and his hands start to sweat. Megan was the only woman who'd caused that type of reaction.

While he stood there gaping, she put the tickets into her tiny purse and picked up a silver wrap made of some sort of gauzy fabric and started to put it around her shoulders. Cade snapped out of his daze when he realized what she was doing. "Let me help you with that."

"Thanks." Her smile was brilliant, and the warmth from her voice reached places in his heart he'd believed were frozen solid and would never thaw. He'd been wrong. Even now he heard the ice cracking and sensed the coldness in him was beginning to warm. The feeling wasn't unpleasant and he wondered if it was love that was responsible for the change.

Not that he was in love with Megan. That would be impossible after such a short time. He'd been fooled by infatuation once before and rashly proposed marriage to the wrong woman. He was wiser now. But still this didn't feel like infatuation. It felt like love. And what was he going to do if it actually was?

Megan glanced at Cade from the side of her eye. Something was wrong although she couldn't imagine what. Cade had seemed perfectly normal when he'd picked her up. He'd smiled at her, then had gone mute.

It seemed as if he had checked out. Oh, he'd nodded a couple of times when she spoke to him, and his glazed eyes had even cleared up for a few seconds on a couple of occasions. But that was it.

She mentally replayed everything she'd said from the time she'd locked her door behind them to the time they'd gotten into his car, looking for something that she'd done that might have offended him. Nothing came to mind. Another mile passed in silence. If this kept up, they'd arrive at the hotel without a word being spoken between them for the entire drive.

Over the years she'd learned to tolerate uncomfortable silences, but that didn't mean she liked them. And she certainly didn't want to endure one on what was supposed to be a fun date. If the evening went according to plan, she and Cade would be enjoying dinner and hopefully dancing for the next few hours. She didn't want the night to be a chore for either of them.

Perhaps he regretted agreeing to come with her. If that was the case, tonight was going to be awkward. She just wished he had said something sooner. Megan exhaled and told herself to calm down. Before she jumped to conclusions, she needed to broach the subject just to be sure she wasn't misinterpreting his silence. "Thanks for agreeing to come with me. We don't have to stay long if you'd prefer we didn't."

Cade took his eyes off the road for a brief second while he looked over at her. "I'm happy to come, though I have to admit that I don't usually attend this type of function."

Maybe he was just nervous. She could relate. "Me

neither. But it is fun to dress up once in a while and do something different."

He smiled. "And if I haven't told you yet, you look lovely."

"Thanks. You look rather dashing yourself."

"*Dashing*. There's a word that's never been used to describe me before."

"Maybe not to your face."

He laughed. "You have me there. Who knows what people say behind my back."

Megan laughed with him. If only he knew the words she used earlier this week to describe him to her friends back home in New York. After hearing Megan's description, Kayla had been ready to jump in her car and see the type of men they grew in the South. Paula had wanted to see him for herself as well, but she'd been willing to settle for the picture Megan promised to take tonight.

Now that the ice had been broken, Cade and Megan talked comfortably for the rest of the drive. When they reached their destination, Cade parked and then led her inside the hotel. They took a few steps inside the cavernous lobby and Cade let out a low whistle. "Nice."

"Very." The marble floor and paneled walls were exquisite. Enormous bouquets in crystal vases added color and made the space feel more elegant.

They found the ballroom easily enough. After handing their tickets to a distinguished gentleman at the door, they went inside the ballroom. Dozens of round tables filled the space. Megan said, "We're at table eleven."

They skirted the tables until they found theirs. Cade held her chair before sitting beside her. Two other couples were already seated and they all introduced themselves. When the others discovered Megan had recently moved to town from New York, they began to tell her the places she should visit. They told her about hole-in-the-wall restaurants that served the best food and neighborhood shops selling original jewelry and artwork. Megan made a mental note to visit several of the places mentioned in the near future.

The conversation flowed from there to sports to movies and Megan enjoyed herself immensely. She exchanged numbers and business cards with the women, and they made plans to get together in the coming weeks. Though she had only known them for a few hours, Megan had the feeling that they would become good friends. The decision to move to North Carolina was looking better and better every day.

Dinner was delicious, and once they'd finished dessert and coffee, the jazz quintet that had played throughout the meal was replaced by a DJ. The first song he played was greeted with cheers, and the tables emptied as most people headed to the dance floor. Megan glanced at Cade, hoping against hope that he knew how to dance. He flashed a dimpled smile in response to her unasked question and held out a hand. Thank goodness.

After the first couple of dances, Megan became more intrigued. Who was this man? He was kind to animals and loved and respected his father. He was a great cook, and now it turned out that he was a fabulous dancer, too. Cade had moves so smooth he glided from dance to dance without missing a beat. Eventually the up-tempo songs ended and the DJ played a slow one. When he held open his arms, Megan stepped into them without hesitation. His arms closed around her bare back and she shivered at his gentle touch. She leaned her head against his shoulder and inhaled. Though Cade's cologne was positively dreamy, it was his own unique scent that made her knees weak.

As they moved to the sultry saxophone, Megan's imagination began to fire up. What would it be like for Cade to hold her close even when they weren't dancing? How good would it feel to be loved by a man like Cade? Though he called himself a simple farmer, in truth, he was a complex man. He was kind and gentle even though he had rough edges. There were moments when he understood her like no one ever had and times when he confused her to no end. There was a confidence and stillness to him that gave her a peace she hadn't felt for fourteen years. There was a depth to him that had her wanting to know more about him. Simply stated, Cade was everything she wanted in a man.

"Are you having a good time?" he asked. His lips were near her ear and his warm breath had goose bumps popping out on her arms.

She looked up at him. Although she'd enjoyed every second of the night, nothing compared to the pleasure she felt in this moment. She wished she could stay wrapped in his arms forever. "Yes. You?"

"This is the best time I've had in a while." He spun her around. "Thanks for inviting me."

Megan nodded. "Thanks for saying yes."

They danced to every song, and Megan sighed when

the DJ announced that the next song would be the last. Where had the time gone?

"I hope he plays the fifteen-minute disco version," Cade said.

Megan laughed. "Or the twenty-minute mix tape."

"But just in case he doesn't, we'd better make the best of the next three minutes," Cade said, as he pulled Megan even closer. His heart beat rapidly beneath her ear, pounding in time with her own. She closed her eyes and let the music carry her away. It seemed like only seconds before the music stopped and the DJ thanked everyone for supporting such a worthy cause. He announced the amount they'd raised at the silent auction, and Megan gasped and joined in the applause. The organizers had exceeded their goal by almost ten percent. They returned to their table and said their goodbyes.

Megan and Cade held hands as they walked through the parking lot. It felt so natural to have his hand wrapped around hers. She could totally get used to this. Megan hummed as Cade pulled the car into the street.

"I guess we don't need the radio," Cade joked.

"Oh, yes we do. You might not have noticed, but I've been humming the same three notes over and over."

"I noticed. And might I say that you mastered them. Another few dates and you'll be able to hum the entire song."

Megan's heart stopped. Was Cade hinting that he wanted to go on more dates? Or was he just kidding with her? Since this had been such a magical night, she was going to choose to believe the former. She was definitely ready for another night spent with him.

When they arrived at her house, he parked and then helped her from the car. Her heart was thumping a crazy beat as they walked hand in hand to her front door. He waited patiently while she unlocked it. Suddenly shy, she smiled up at him. "I had a great time."

"So did I." His voice was husky and her stomach swooped like crazy. He lowered his head and kissed her. At the first contact, her knees wobbled and she wrapped her arms around his neck and held on for dear life. He deepened the kiss and she responded eagerly. She didn't know how much time passed, but when he pulled back she was breathing hard. He pressed his forehead against hers. "Wow. I need to get going."

Though she didn't want him to leave, she knew it was the right thing for now. They were still getting to know each other. At this stage in their relationship, they didn't need to confuse things. "I'll see you tomorrow."

"Sleep in if you want. I'll take care of feeding the pets in the morning."

"Thanks." But as she watched him drive away, she knew she wouldn't be sleeping anytime soon. Not when she could relive the night they'd just shared, especially that earth-shattering kiss that had hinted at a promise for the future.

Chapter Fourteen

Megan's heart thumped with excitement as she got ready to go to the farm the next afternoon. She'd taken Cade up on his offer to feed the remaining animals that morning, using the extra time to catch up on a few things at home. She'd cleaned the house from front to back and done three loads of laundry. Now the housework was done, so she hopped into her car and drove the now familiar route to the farm.

When she arrived, Cade was inside the corral, tossing balls to the dogs. As usual, Samson was the only cat in sight. Over the past week, more cats and dogs had gone to the shelter, so now only two dogs and three cats remained. Megan still missed them, but she was happy that they were finding their forever homes. Gumball and Tiny, for example, had both been adopted by a family with eight-year-old twin boys. But as the animals moved to the shelter, she knew that she would soon lose her reason to come out to the farm every day. Would she and Cade continue to see each other once all of the animals found new homes?

It was amazing how quickly an obligation had become something she enjoyed having in her life. Megan loved all of the remaining animals and would watch them leave with mixed emotions, but it would break her heart to say goodbye to Samson and Delilah. Cade felt the same way, so they'd agreed that Samson and Delilah would be the last ones taken to the shelter. Megan didn't know if she had the right, but she was going to insist that they be adopted together. They'd created their own family and it would be wrong to separate them.

"Hey," Cade called, tossing the ball one last time before crossing the corral. When he reached the fence, he climbed up and sat on the top rail. He gestured for her to join him so she did. For a moment they sat in companionable silence and just watched the dogs play.

Megan closed her eyes and soaked in the peace of the farm. With the noise the animals made—the clucking of the chickens, the chirping of the birds, and the mooing of the cows—it wasn't exactly quiet. But these sounds, accompanied by the gentle breeze, soothed her soul. She looked forward to coming here each day after work and didn't want to think of the time when it would no longer be necessary.

"Have you made up your mind about buying your house?" Cade asked after a while. The fact that he'd mentioned *that* when she was thinking about how much she enjoyed being on the farm was jarring.

"Yes. I don't think I'm going to buy it." She'd thought long and hard about the decision before concluding that it wasn't the right thing for her. Although she liked the house, it didn't have room for a family. Buying the house felt like she was resigning herself to being alone for the rest of her life. She hadn't given up hope of having a family of her own one day.

"No?"

His voice was a combination of surprise and something close to disappointment.

"I don't think it's right for me."

He nodded but didn't say anything. The silence stretched on, but it wasn't the relaxed silence they'd shared only moments ago. Megan's nerves grew taut as the tense silence stretched from one minute to the next.

Finally she turned to him. "What's wrong?"

Instead of looking at her, he directed his focus to the animals. "I've been thinking."

"About?" she asked when he didn't say anything else.

"The cats and dogs. I talked to Rebekah today. She'll have room for the other animals by Saturday. We're down to a handful now. I can take care of them on my own without too much trouble until then."

"What are you saying?" Her heart was sinking to her toes, but she wanted him to be clear. She didn't want there to be any misunderstanding.

"You don't need to come out here every day to feed and clean up after them. I can handle it on my own."

"You don't have to do that. I made the promise to Mrs. Crockett, not you. Of course I'm going to keep it."

"You promised that they would be well cared for, not that you would personally wait on them. And you know they're in great hands here. They're living the life."

She folded her hands and lifted her chin, steeling herself for what she knew would be coming. After all, this wasn't the first time she'd heard the words. She just wondered what line he would use. Would he tell her that it was best for her that they stop seeing each other? Or would he go with the one where he'd say they were just too different? Maybe he'd blame her for something she hadn't done? Not that it mattered. The underlying truth would remain.

He didn't want her.

"What are you really saying, Cade? If you don't want me to come around, then just say that. I can handle it."

He blew out a breath. "That's rather harsh, don't you think?"

"It's direct," she corrected him. Flowery words wouldn't alter the message. "Are you ending things between us? Of course, that's assuming there was something between us in the first place. We might have kissed a few times, but we never made any type of commitment to each other. But still, I need to know. What do you mean? Do you want a relationship with me, or are you sending me on my merry way?"

Cade breathed deeply and reminded himself to stay strong. No matter how she tried to twist things, *Megan* was the one who refused to commit. She'd said it plainly. They'd only kissed a few times, which to her way of thinking didn't constitute a relationship—not to her. It had meant something to him. But then he was a small-town farmer. Maybe big-city women looked at things differently than he did. His former fiancée was proof of that. He should have learned his lesson then, but he hadn't. It would hurt him to do so, but he needed to get Megan out of his life now. He would do it fast and get the pain over with. Like ripping off a Band-Aid.

"I think we might have ignored a couple of red flags. Sure, we had a lot of fun taking care of the animals and going to that fundraiser last night, but we're too different. We want different things."

Megan looked at him. "I understand. I love Samson. I don't think he and Delilah should be separated. I would take them both but I don't have a fenced-in yard. Please don't let Rebekah allow them to be separated."

"They won't be. I've decided to keep Delilah. I figured you would want Samson."

"Not if it means separating them. They love each other and should be together."

"I agree. I'll keep them together."

"Thanks." Megan slid from the rail. The minute her feet hit the ground she walked to her car. She didn't stop to talk to Reginald like she usually did. She did bend over and pick up Samson, giving the cat a hug and kiss before she set him down and got into her car. A minute later she was gone from his life.

"It's for the best," Cade told himself. Megan wasn't a farm girl and she would never be happy here. They'd be better off with other people. And the ache in his heart that made breathing next to impossible? It was to be expected. Wasn't that what you felt when you fell in love with someone who wasn't in love with you?

Cade jumped from the rail and back into the corral. Maybe playing with the dogs would help him ignore the hurt that came from losing something very precious. After tossing the ball so many times he thought his arm would fall off, he fed the animals, then went into his father's kitchen. On the way, he checked his phone to see if Megan had texted to let him know she'd arrived home safely. She hadn't. But then, why would she? They weren't dating. Whatever had been between them was over.

"Where's Megan?" Reginald asked, turning from the stove. "I thought I heard her car."

"She's gone and she won't be coming back. I told her I don't need her help."

Reginald gave Cade a long, wordless look before stirring the gravy and turning off the stove. His father muttered to himself while they prepared their plates. Cade readied himself for the lecture he knew was coming. And Reginald didn't disappoint. Once they were seated across from each other, Reginald looked Cade dead in the eye. "You're being a fool."

"That's your opinion." Cade wouldn't disrespect his father, but he really didn't want to have this conversation.

"How long are you going to let Deadra control your life?"

"Deadra? What does she have to do with anything? I'm totally over her. I have been for a while."

"You might not be thinking about her or talking about her, and you may even be over her, but that girl is still in your head. She controls everything you do. Or rather, everything you don't do."

"Meaning?" Cade put down his fork. His appetite had begun to shrink the minute his father started talking, growing smaller with every word. Now Cade couldn't choke down a bite.

"*Meaning* you've painted Megan with the same brush as you did Deadra. You keep comparing Megan to her even though the two couldn't be more different."

"I wouldn't say that. They're both from big cities. Neither one of them had stepped foot on a farm until they came here."

"Those things don't matter. That could describe any number of people. But when it comes to their hearts and what will make them happy in the long run, they are night and day. Deadra wasn't going to be happy living here. It's much too quiet and slow. She was just more suited to city life. Some people are. Just as you're more suited to life on the farm. Neither place is better than the other. Neither type of person is better than the other."

"I never said anything different."

"No. But you think that because Megan is from the city, she can't be happy with life on the farm with you. And you're wrong."

Cade didn't answer. He wished his father was right, but it wasn't Reginald's heart on the line. Cade wasn't willing to take the risk. His heart wouldn't be able to stand rejection twice in such a short period of time.

Reginald didn't seem to need a reply. Cade knew

his father. Once he'd said what he'd needed to say, he would let the matter drop. It was up to Cade to decide what he would do with his father's words of wisdom.

Reginald pointed his fork. "If you're not going to eat, wrap up your food and take it with you."

Nodding, Cade rose and did just that. Then he went outside, loaded Samson and Delilah into his truck and went home. Sleep took a long time coming. When it finally arrived, it was restless.

The next couple of days were lonely ones for Cade. More than once he'd caught himself looking over his shoulder, hoping he'd see Megan's car coming down the driveway. He never did. And he'd dropped off the last of the animals to the shelter this morning. He'd already told Rebekah he intended to adopt Samson and Delilah and she'd been delighted. He was happy with his decision, but he would have been happier if he and Megan could be together as well.

He'd come close to calling her on several occasions, but had stopped himself. What would be the point? Megan wasn't willing to commit to him and he didn't want to settle for less.

Megan grabbed the mail, then trudged into her house. These past days had been so hard. She felt so empty without Cade. For the first time in a while, she'd felt lonely in her own home. Though he'd only been to her house a couple of times, Megan missed Cade's presence. In order to keep from thinking of him, she'd taken on a few pro bono clients, hoping to help others avoid Mrs. Crockett's fate. She'd begun staying at the office much later than she had in the past. But tonight Daniel had insisted that she leave the office at a normal hour, and he'd made it clear that he wouldn't take no for an answer.

She changed out of her suit and into a pair of shorts and a T-shirt, then sorted the mail. There was a small package, which she saved for last. She knew what it was and her heart ached at the thought of opening it.

Before she and Cade had broken up, she'd ordered matching collars for Samson and Delilah. She'd hoped they would be adopted together and that their collars would be like friendship bracelets. Since Cade had decided to adopt them, they would be together, just as they should be. But she wasn't involved in their lives anymore.

When she'd purchased the collars, things had been going well between her and Cade, and she'd believed she would be a part of his life, too. That hadn't happened. Even so, she still wanted Samson and Delilah to have the collars. She just needed to deliver them.

Before he'd ended things with her, Megan would have simply driven to the farm unannounced. After all, she'd spent nearly as many waking hours there as she had in her own home. But things had changed and she wasn't certain she would be welcome. Though Cade hadn't thrown her off his property, he'd told her he didn't want her there anymore. He'd been clear about that when he'd told her he no longer needed her help with Mrs. Crockett's pets. She would get permission to bring the collars to the farm. Hopefully he would let her.

She grabbed her phone. Her finger trembled as it hovered over Cade's name. Finally she pressed the icon and listened nervously as the phone rang. Breathing became difficult as she waited for him to answer. What if he didn't answer? What if he didn't want to talk to her? Then what?

"Megan?"

The sound of his voice saying her name sent shivers down her spine. She wondered how long it would be before she was truly over him. Hopefully it wouldn't take long. She didn't think she could take much more of the heartache. "Yes."

"Is everything okay?"

"What? Yes. I'm fine." She sighed. "I'd ordered collars for Samson and Delilah. They came in the mail today and I was wondering if I could bring them out to the farm."

"Of course."

"When would be good for you?"

"Anytime. Now."

That was unexpected. Relieved, her breathing became normal again. "Okay. I'm on my way."

"Megan…"

"Yes."

"Drive carefully."

She heard the concern in his voice, and though she told herself that he didn't mean anything by it, her heart still lifted. Maybe he still cared about her.

As Megan drove down the highway, anticipation had the blood racing through her veins. The past few days she'd told herself that she was over Cade, but she knew that wasn't true. She missed him and wanted him in her life. She loved Cade in a way she'd never loved another man and suspected she always would.

Megan parked her car in her usual space and walked to the corral. She expected to see Samson and Delilah, but the corral was empty. She leaned against the rail and waited. Maybe Cade went somewhere and had taken them with him. His truck was parked in its usual spot, so they couldn't have gone far. She climbed on the top rail of the fence and decided to wait. Inhaling a lungful of air, she felt the tranquility of the farm begin to work its magic. The tension she'd brought with her eased and she felt her shoulders relax. She closed her eyes, and for a moment, all felt right in her world.

She heard a sound, opened her eyes and turned. Cade was running from the barn, Delilah at his heels. Cade was calling Samson's name. Megan hopped from the fence and ran over. "What's wrong? What happened?"

Cade looked at her with worried eyes. "We can't find Samson. He was in the yard when you and I talked, but when I turned around and he was gone."

"Surely he has to be around here somewhere." Megan's heart raced and she was consumed with fear. She couldn't lose Samson like this. They had to find him. "Where have you looked?"

"The barn. The corral. I even went to the spot where we found the other cats that time. He wasn't there."

"Did you check your house? Maybe he wanted to go home."

"That was one of the first places I looked. He's not there."

"Did you check the cat mansions?"

"We donated the mansions to the shelter."

Megan spun in a slow circle, hoping to spot Samson in a place Cade might have missed. Nothing. She took a deep breath, trying not to panic. Surely Samson had to be near. Megan looked back at Cade. "Where should we look now?"

Cade rubbed his hands down his face then blew out a long breath. Several tense seconds passed before he spoke. "Let's go toward the road."

Megan's heart froze. Although there wasn't much traffic on the road, there were still enough cars to be a danger to the cat. They jogged down the driveway, pausing every few moments to call Samson's name. Although Megan listened hard, hoping to hear meowing, they were always greeted by silence.

When they reached the road, they started toward town. They looked in the high grass and in every place they thought the cat might be. There was no sign of Samson anywhere. After an hour of fruitless searching, Megan's eyes filled with tears. She tried to hold them back but she couldn't. One slipped out and was quickly followed by another. She wiped them away, but they kept falling.

"Don't cry, Megan," Cade said. He put his arms around her shoulder, gently pulling her into his embrace. Unable to stem the tide of her tears, she pressed her face against his chest and began to sob.

"I know I'm silly crying over a cat. Especially one that doesn't even belong to me." But she was crying over more than the cat, and she had a feeling they both knew it. It was just another loss in a lifetime of losses.

She was also crying because her heart was still broken. Even though he was holding her, she'd lost Cade, too.

"We'll find him and everything will be all right. I promise."

She nodded, but she knew it wouldn't be all right again. Nothing would be all right because she and Cade weren't together.

Delilah barked and they jumped. They'd put her in the corral so that she wouldn't get in the way of the search. Not only that, they didn't want to risk her getting lost, too. One lost pet was enough. But somehow she had managed to get out of the corral and was now charging in their direction. When she reached them she barked and then began trotting down the road ahead of them.

"Delilah," Cade called.

The dog didn't stop or even turn around. Every few steps she'd sniff and then take off again. Cade and Megan looked at each other and then began to follow Delilah. After twenty minutes it became clear that they were headed toward town and Megan's house. They began to call Samson's name again. After a while, they were met with meows and purring. Delilah barked and then raced ahead to a stand of trees. Megan and Cade ran as fast as they could. When they reached the trees, Delilah and Samson were sitting side by side.

"Samson!" Megan ran the last few yards and then dropped to her knees. Laughing through her tears, she scooped the cat into her arms and cradled him against her chest. Tears fell again, but these were tears of joy.

"I was so worried about you. So worried. Don't ever run away again. I don't think I could take it."

As Cade watched the reunion he realized that his heart was beating hard. For the first time in days the emptiness inside him was gone. He knew his heart was full because Megan was back on the farm. Though he'd fought the emotion with everything inside him, he'd missed her. The farm had been too quiet and colorless without her. She'd brought the life back with her.

Megan and Samson were so happy to be reunited. They belonged together. He could be a part of their unit if he was bold enough to take the step. And truly, it wasn't that big of a risk. Megan cared about him. He knew that now. Maybe he'd always known it. She might not be willing to buy a house now, but that didn't mean she had one foot out of town. His father had been right. Cade had been looking at everything Megan did or didn't do through the lens of Deadra. Seeing the way Megan was holding on to Samson for dear life, it occurred to him that Megan and Deadra weren't alike in the ways that mattered. They were two different people who had different needs and wants.

Deciding that he was not going to let Megan leave again, he walked up to her and wrapped her in his arms. It felt so good to hold her. If she'd let him, he'd hold her there for the rest of their lives. "He's okay."

"I know. I was just so worried. I don't want to let him go again."

"I understand that feeling."

Megan looked at him and smiled. "I'm sorry. I've

been hogging him. I know you were worried. I guess you want to hold him, too."

"I was worried, but that's not what I meant. I meant I don't want to let you go again."

Megan froze, her hand in the air. "What?"

"I love you, Megan. I want you in my life."

"What?" She shook her head. "Say that again. I must have misheard."

He smiled then took her hand into his. "You heard right. I love you."

"You love me."

He nodded.

"Since when?"

"I don't know. It just kind of sneaked up on me. I tried to fight it because I was scared."

"Of what?"

"Of being hurt again. I let my fear get the best of me and I ended up hurting you instead. I'm sorry."

Megan's eyes widened and she pressed a hand against her breast. "I don't understand. If you love me then why did you send me away? This is just your relief talking. You already told me that you don't want me."

Didn't want her? Where did she get that crazy idea? "I do want you."

"Why did you want me to buy the house if you want me?"

He shook his head. "I wanted you to buy the house so you would stay in town. I thought if you had something to hold you here, you wouldn't leave Spring Forest. Or me."

"Oh. I thought you were letting me know that you didn't want me on the farm. At least not permanently.

And then you even told me not to come back to the farm to help care for the pets."

How could he have been so stupid? He should have known Megan would think that. She'd had more than one family send her away. In her eyes he was doing the same. "I want you. Do you think you could be happy living out here? We're so far from everything."

"Of course I can. And you're not that far away from what I want most."

"And that's what?"

"You. A family of my own. I love you, too."

He smiled and kissed her lips. He felt the wholeness that had been missing for a while. "In that case, let's get back home."

They stood and he wrapped his arm around her waist. As they turned and headed for the house, Megan spotted something in the trees. "What's that? Is that a lost dog?"

Cade took a few steps in the dog's direction, walking slowly so as not to scare him. The little dirty gray dog barked once and ran through the trees. Cade chased after it for a minute, but the dog was too fast for him. Returning to Megan, he shook his head. "I couldn't catch him. We're not the only ones who've tried. From what I hear, many people have seen him, but no one has been able to catch him."

"I hope he'll be all right. He needs a family to take care of him."

"I know. And I hope he will find one, just like we have."

Megan smiled. "Just like we have."

* * * * *

*Look for the next book in Furever Yours
the new Special Edition continuity*

A Small-Town Baby Surprise
by Christy Jeffries

*On sale June 2019, wherever
Harlequin books and ebooks are sold.*

And fetch the previous Furever Yours tales!

The Nanny Clause
by USA TODAY *Bestselling Author*
Karen Rose Smith

Not Just the Girl Next Door
by Stacy Connelly

Available now!

Get 4 FREE REWARDS!

We'll send you 2 FREE Books plus 2 FREE Mystery Gifts.

AMERICAN HEROES

The Captains' Vegas Vows

Caro Carson

SPECIAL EDITION

Almost a Bravo

Christine Rimmer

Harlequin® Special Edition books feature heroines finding the balance between their work life and personal life on the way to finding true love.

FREE Value Over $20

SPECIAL EXCERPT FROM

H HARLEQUIN®

SPECIAL EDITION

*Losing Miranda broke Matt Grimes's heart.
And kept him from the knowledge of his pending
fatherhood. Now Miranda Contreras has returned
to Rocking Chair, Texas—with their eight-year-old
daughter. Matt should be angry! What other secrets
could Miranda be keeping? But all he sees is a chance
to be the family they were meant to be.*

Read on for a sneak preview of
The Cowboy's Secret Family,
the next great book in USA TODAY *bestselling author
Judy Duarte's Rocking Chair Rodeo miniseries.*

When Matt looked up, she offered him a shy smile. "Like
I said, I'm sorry. I should have told you that you were a
father."

"You've got that right."

"I've made mistakes, but Emily isn't one of them.
She's a great kid. So for now, let's focus on her."

"All right." Matt uncrossed his arms and raked a hand
through his hair. "But just for the record, I would've done
anything in my power to take care of you and Emily."

"I know." And that was why she'd walked away from
him. Matt would have stood up to her father, challenged
his threat, only to be knocked to his knees—and worse.

No, leaving town and cutting all ties with Matt was the
only thing she could've done to protect him.

As she stood in the room where their daughter was conceived, as she studied the only man she'd ever loved, the memories crept up on her…the old feelings, too.

When she was sixteen, there'd been something about the fun-loving nineteen-year-old cowboy that had drawn her attention. And whatever it was continued to tug at her now. But she shook it off. Too many years had passed; too many tears had been shed.

Besides, an unwed single mother who was expecting another man's baby wouldn't stand a chance with a champion bull rider who had his choice of pretty cowgirls. And she'd best not forget that.

"Aw, hell," Matt said, as he ran a hand through his hair again and blew out a weary sigh. "Maybe you did Emily a favor by leaving when you did. Who knows what kind of father I would have made back then. Or even now."

Don't miss
The Cowboy's Secret Family *by Judy Duarte,*
available June 2019 wherever
Harlequin® Special Edition books and ebooks are sold.

www.Harlequin.com

Looking for more satisfying love stories
with community and family at their core?

Check out **Harlequin® Special Edition**
and **Love Inspired®** books!

New books available every month!

CONNECT WITH US AT:

Facebook.com/groups/HarlequinConnection

 Facebook.com/HarlequinBooks

Twitter.com/HarlequinBooks

 Instagram.com/HarlequinBooks

Pinterest.com/HarlequinBooks

ReaderService.com

**ROMANCE WHEN
YOU NEED IT**

HFGENRE2018

Love Harlequin romance?

DISCOVER.

Be the first to find out about promotions, news and exclusive content!

 Facebook.com/HarlequinBooks

Twitter.com/HarlequinBooks

 Instagram.com/HarlequinBooks

Pinterest.com/HarlequinBooks

ReaderService.com

EXPLORE.

Sign up for the Harlequin e-newsletter and download a free book from any series at **TryHarlequin.com.**

CONNECT.

Join our Harlequin community to share your thoughts and connect with other romance readers!
Facebook.com/groups/HarlequinConnection

**ROMANCE WHEN
YOU NEED IT**

HSOCIAL2018